A FIST AROUND THE HEART

PRAISE FOR A FIST AROUND THE HEART

"*A Fist Around the Heart* is a compelling and powerful tale permeated with a longing for what can never be. Chisvin's beautifully realized characters, the independent Anna and her fragile sister Esther, reflect not only the vulnerability of the human condition but also its tenacity."

–Linda Hutsell-Manning
That Summer in Franklin

"*A Fist Around the Heart* features multi-national settings, rich historical details about everything from contraception to pogroms and much else—and, at its heart, the profound effects of an improbable true incident—If Day. An illuminating look at family ties and the reverberating effects of European violence against Jews before World War II."

–Carlyn Zwarenstein
Opium Eater: The New Confessions

A • FIST AROUND • THE • HEART

HEATHER CHISVIN

Second Story Press

Library and Archives Canada Cataloguing in Publication

Chisvin, Heather, author
A fist around the heart / Heather Chisvin.

Issued in print and electronic formats.
ISBN 978-1-77260-066-7 (softcover).--ISBN 978-1-77260-065-0 (HTML)

I. Title.

PS8605.H587F57 2018   C813'.6   C2017-907066-5
                                              C2017-907067-
ISBN Paperback: 978-1-77260-065-0
ISBN E-book: 978-1-77260-066-7

Printed and bound in Canada

A Note on Language
Use of language in this book should be viewed in the context of its time in history. The
author and publisher do not condone inappropriate or disrespectful language.

*Second Story Press gratefully acknowledges the support of the
Ontario Arts Council and the Canada Council for the Arts for our
publishing program. We acknowledge the financial support of the
Government of Canada through the Canada Book Fund.*

ONTARIO ARTS COUNCIL
CONSEIL DES ARTS DE L'ONTARIO
an Ontario government agency
un organisme du gouvernement de l'Ontario

Funded by the Government of Canada
Financé par le gouvernement du Canada

Canada Council   Conseil des Arts
for the Arts   du Canada

MIX
Paper from
responsible sources
FSC® C004071

Published by
SECOND STORY PRESS
20 Maud Street, Suite 401
Toronto, ON M5V 2M5
www.secondstorypress.ca

• FOR KURT •

AND FOR ELENA AND HAZEL

Maybe all one can do is hope to end up with the right regrets.

—Arthur Miller, *The Crucible*

*E*sther is in her room again, crying.
I can see it still so clearly.

I knock softly on her door. "Esther, may I come in?"

The crying stops. I imagine she's lifting her tear-streaked face from the pillow and turning to the door. "I'll be fine, Bencke," she says. "You don't have to wait there."

She won't be fine. I know that now about my sister. I also know that she will, sooner or later, let me in, so I slide slowly down the wall and pull my knees up to my chest, hoping the Countess doesn't come by and see me sitting like this.

I begin stroking the green velvet runner that Brigitte has just brushed to a fine pile and start counting. One hundred and fifty strokes takes about five minutes. At five hundred I get up and walk to the tall window that overlooks the back of the estate. Yellow leaves are skimming along the riverbank. Moses is turning his wagon around at the kitchen entrance and heading for the main road, his egg baskets knocking gently against each other. I had hoped to put on my boys' clothes and sneak out on his rounds with him, but it's too late now.

I go back to Esther's closed door, slide down the wall again, and wait until she lets me in.

"It happened again, Bencke," she says when we're settled on her bed, my back against the puffy velvet headboard, her head in my lap.

1

"*What happened, Esther?*"

I know of course what happened. I also know that it calms her to have me there, so we sit, the sun seeping in around the edges of the closed curtains, outlining a room that's larger than our whole house had been in Russia. I brush the moist strands of hair from her face, her blond tendrils dark with tears. I had so wanted to go around the city with Moses. I would have climbed up beside him and held the reins, clucking at Ron to go or stop or turn, leaves and gravel crunching under the wagon wheels.

"*Will you be all right, Esther?*" *I ask.*

I must have asked her that question a thousand times. I asked when I was seven and she was eleven. I asked when I was eleven and she was fifteen. I asked until I couldn't bear asking anymore. I still don't know which was harder, not asking and not knowing, or asking and hearing her answer, "*Sometimes I'm afraid I'll die of this.*"

• CHAPTER ONE •

They say you can't remember things that happen before you're seven or eight. I know that's not true. I was only five when everything changed, and I have clear memories of that day in Russia: the smell of the laundry in Mamma's basket as I helped her carry it outside; my stocky little legs taking three steps to her every one. Esther's long legs flashing by us on her way to the swing. If my memory isn't playing tricks on me, I can even recall how the air felt that day.

We were in the dirt yard between our house and Nathaniel's. It was more mud than dirt and our boots were sinking in, but I didn't care. None of us did. We were just so happy to be outside after ten days of such torrential rain that Mamma hadn't been able to walk to the castle to do the Countess's sewing.

Esther kicked her boots off when she got to the swing and started pumping, the ropes of the swing creaking as she leaned backward and forward, eager to become level with the crossbar.

Mamma set the laundry basket down in front of the line between the two pines and began her ritual—bending, lifting, reaching, the bag of clothes pegs on her wrist sliding up and down her arm. I stood close, ready with the next piece of laundry, proud that I could help.

When Nathaniel came out of his house with his bag of marbles, I ran to join him. We sat facing each other under the big pine, legs straight out, feet touching so the marbles wouldn't stray, little drops of water collecting on the boughs and plopping on our bare heads and hands.

It never occurred to me that the deep pleasure of that day—Mamma and Esther and Nathaniel close, the little cemetery behind us, the gently sloping hills in the distance, the feeling that everything was as it should be—could ever change.

"Anit!" We heard Fat Amos calling to Mamma before we saw him. "Anit!" He was having trouble breathing by the time he reached her.

We turned to look at him, Esther and Nathaniel and I, waiting to hear what he would say next. Glancing over at us briefly, he put his head close to hers and began speaking in the voice grown-ups used when they didn't want us to hear.

The sheet fell from Mamma's hands.

I know now what day that was, what Amos told Mamma. It was March 13, 1881. He told her that our tsar had just been assassinated; that the Jews were being blamed and they were searching all the shtetls. Mamma knew ours wouldn't be long.

Things were never the same after that. Mamma stopped humming and started jumping at sudden noises. She and Pappa began whispering at night. I imagine now that she was begging him not to leave Podensk to find work, telling him that it wasn't safe anymore for Jews to leave their shtetls. He continued to leave though. I suppose the repercussions of not making a living for his family were worse for him than his fear of being caught.

They put on a good face in front of Esther and me, though, pretending everything was fine, but I could tell it wasn't.

Even a few weeks later, when they brought Pappa home lying on a door and put him in bed, they acted like nothing was wrong. Mamma made a game of serving Esther and me breakfast in bed with him. At night, she would set a candle on a chair beside his bed and Pappa would make shadow animals on the wall with his hands and ask us what they were, what kind of sound they made.

And then came that cold day in October when Mamma woke us earlier than usual to go to the castle with her. Pappa asked her to leave us with him, told her that we would have fun, but she told him that she needed us to help carry the Countess's satchel, that it was heavy with her sewing.

I knew that wasn't true. I had watched Mamma the night before. She got out of bed when Pappa started snoring, put the Countess's green satchel on the table, and started putting what looked like Esther's and my clothes in it. She stopped at one point, pulled her chair out quietly, and tiptoed to the cot where Esther and I slept. I made my eyes into slits so she wouldn't know I was awake. She reached up into one of the baskets on the shelf above our cot and took out the book that Esther had made for my third birthday, *Pappa's Pockets*.

* * *

I have the book still on the bottom shelf of the big glass coffee table in my office. The bright yellow cover is a dull ochre now, and the leaves Esther glued on and painted over with pine resin are gravelly little bumps.

It's our story really, about two sisters who live in a small village with their mamma and pappa. The pappa builds houses and furniture for rich people and is often away. When he comes home he always has treats in his pockets, one for his little daughter, one for his big daughter, and one for the mamma. But before he gives anyone their treat, they have to guess which of his pockets it is in. "Is it in that pocket, Pappa?" they ask. "Is it in that one?" The game goes on until the right pocket is found and the gifts revealed. Pappa brought home sweets and smooth rocks, a potato once that looked like their uncle Zalman, a spoon, some wool and thread for Mamma. One day his jacket pocket was jiggling when he came in and before anyone could say anything, he lifted out a tiny, white, mewling kitten. After that, he always brought a treat for the kitten too.

* * *

My eyelids heavy that night, I watched Mamma put *Pappa's Pockets* in the satchel with Esther's and my clothes and take it to the door. She went back to the table then, put her arms on the table and her head on her arms. I think now that she slept there all night so she wouldn't wake Pappa and have to explain what she was doing.

* * *

Esther and I loved going to the castle with Mamma. We played in a big room off the kitchen while Mamma did her sewing upstairs for Countess Chernovski. The Count, a slim, handsome man with a pointed beard, came down sometimes and told us stories about growing up in the castle. He knew every tunnel and tower and promised that he would take me through them all one day when I was big enough. The Countess came down sometimes with Mamma. They would sit and have tea.

Mamma had a privileged position at the castle, I realize now. She was the only servant allowed to live at home. When she and Pappa married, the Countess gave her enough fine fabric to cover a duvet and make a curtain around their bed for privacy. Every Christmas she gave us gift baskets. There was a wooden puppet with a long red hat inside my basket one year; a small box with small gold hoop earrings in Esther's. I think we stayed over at Chernovski Castle one Christmas Eve. I remember a long table, shinier than ours at home, with skinny white candles, eggs in silver cups, and tiny spoons to eat them.

I could be making that up. Mamma said I made up a lot of things or dreamed them.

* * *

We left the house early the morning after I stayed up to watch Mamma pack the satchel. She didn't want to be late, she said, so we hurried with our heavy sweaters and scarves. Most of the leaves were gone from the trees by then so we could see the fat-cheeked chipmunks leaping from branch to branch. In the stream, the fish were leaping too, leaving little silver arcs on the water.

Esther and I walked in front of Mamma, holding hands and bumping hips with every other step like we always did. Esther was teaching me to count: One bump, two bumps, three bumps, four. Even though I was only five, I could count up to thirty.

When we got to the path that led to the castle, Esther and I turned in, but Mamma walked past it. In her quiet voice, she told us to stay close. I glanced up at Esther to see what was going on, but she wouldn't look at me. She held my hand more tightly and we walked much farther, all the way to the train stop.

I was tired by the time we got there, but excited. I thought maybe our cousins from St. Petersburg were coming for a visit, but it was the Count who stepped down from the train, not our cousins. He picked me up with one hand, put his other hand on Esther's back, and walked us up a little step stool to a small wood-paneled compartment on the train. The Countess stood up when we came in and lifted two chamois

7

bags from the seat beside her. She gave one to Esther and one to me. Esther opened hers and took out a journal, green with gold details at the top corners. She curtsied and said thank you.

I took my bag to the window. When I saw that Mamma was still there, I dropped it and started banging on the window and yelling for her. I was sure they had forgotten her.

* * *

I know I was easy to dislike on that trip. I cried and kicked and hurled myself against the door. I slipped out of the train compartments and ship cabins every time fresh linens or meals were delivered. But in my defense, I was only doing what any five-year-old ripped from her home would have done. I was looking for my mamma. I yearned for the smell of her arms, the sound of her voice telling me not to be afraid of the speed of the train, the vast nothingness of the ocean, but most of all, not to be afraid of the sudden strangeness of Esther's behavior.

Esther wouldn't let me sleep with her anymore. She wouldn't hold me or smooth my hair. She would read to me from *Pappa's Pockets*, but only if I sat very still beside her with my hands in my lap. Now and then, though, she would stop reading, get a vacant look on her face, as if she had forgotten where she was and what she was doing. Sometimes on our way to the washroom, she would collapse against the wall, gripping my hand so tightly it hurt. I could tell she was confused and frightened, which confused and frightened me.

The Countess did her best to console me. So did the Count, but I was inconsolable. When our ship reached Le Havre, none of us could get out of our overheated cabin fast enough.

It was mid-November when we docked, but as warm as a summer day. A few clouds in a calm sky, seagulls swooping in and squawking off when the children got too close. I have pictures the ship's traveling photographer took that bring it all back. A few are of the four of us on the first-class deck; the Count and Countess behind, Esther and I in front in our stiff new high-collared dresses; Esther elegant and slender; me tall and strong-looking, even then. We have a few pictures of our arrival on the wharf that day: men walking with their faces up to the sun; women sitting on the wharf, hands on their oilcloth bundles, eyes on the children running off weeks of pent-up energy.

I ran along with the children chasing the seagulls, delighted to be outside, moving freely. The Count walked with me until I flopped over from exhaustion. He carried me back to the bench where Esther and the Countess were sitting. Taking a seat between them, he spread a map over his lap and traced our route for Esther and the Countess: Podensk, St. Petersburg, Le Havre, Halifax, and finally our new home on Armstrong's Point in Winnipeg. I don't remember all that from the trip, of course. The Count retraced the route for me many times over the years.

I stood in front of them, trying to get the hang of a skipping rope the captain of the steamer had given me. I couldn't do it. The red dress I was wearing was so big and stiff I couldn't see beyond it to my feet so I wandered off, trailing the skipping rope behind me.

I don't think I was looking for Mamma anymore. I had accepted by then that she wasn't with us. I was hoping to find Nathaniel. I knew he had to be around somewhere because we had seen him on the ship a few times coming up from below deck with his family. They climbed up a rope ladder in their underwear, I remember, arms wrapped around their bodies. A deckhand herded them to a corner and sprayed them down with the big black hose they normally used to wash the deck. The little ones and the old ones sometimes fell over.

When I started sneaking into Esther's room and reading her journals a few years later, I saw that her first entry was about the hosing down of the people below deck. It had upset her to see people being treated like animals. The Count told her, she wrote, that it was important that they keep clean, that it cut down on lice and disease. He said he knew it wasn't dignified, but they had hope.

I wonder if Mamma and Pappa will have to travel to us with hope instead of dignity, was what she wrote.

When I got to the end of the wharf, I dropped my skipping rope and looked out over the ocean, wondering how the seagulls could walk on the water. I pulled off one shiny red shoe and threw it in and watched it bob off. I did the same thing with the other shoe. Turning to face the wharf, I backed down a hanging rope ladder, slowly, carefully, tentatively finding each rung with my foot before I put my weight on it.

When I opened my eyes, the Count's face and the Countess's and Esther's were in front of me. Their lips were moving but there were no sounds. The next time I opened my eyes, I was sitting on the Count's lap wrapped in a warm towel. The Countess was on her knees in front of me, a steaming bowl in one hand and a spoon held out to me in the other.

• CHAPTER TWO •

Years later—it was 1942 and I had been living in Manhattan for some time—the Jewish Museum on the Upper East Side mounted an exhibit on Alexander II's assassination that brought back that muddy day in Russia and the days that followed as if they had happened yesterday: Fat Amos running into our yard, the sheet in Mamma's hands falling into the mud, whispers in the night, averted glances, aborted conversations, the sudden, shocking trip to Winnipeg for Esther and me; and, of course, the changes in Esther. For me, from then on, it was always about the changes in Esther.

Esther was visiting with me in Manhattan while the exhibit was on. She was still living in Winnipeg—a widow by then—in a mansion her husband, Charles, had built for her very close to where we had grown up.

I asked her to come to the exhibit with me; I thought she might find it interesting. She refused, saying there was a Cuban artist at a gallery in SoHo that she would rather see. For just a moment I thought I was picking up on her old fears, but I put that aside. I waited until the day after she left for Winnipeg and went to the exhibit with my downstairs tenant and dearest friend, Vera Warsaly.

The tsar's assassination was old news by then. We all knew what had happened and what had followed, but I was interested and thought Vera, who was also born in Russia, would be too.

Even though the museum was almost five miles away, we decided to walk. The streets looked and felt so different than they had a few months earlier when America was still dithering about whether to enter the war. Young men in uniforms were everywhere now. Posters in windows and on walls urged them to do their duty. You could feel an energy and purpose and pride.

The exhibit on Alexander was housed in a high, chalk-white, windowless room at the end of a dark, narrow hallway. The effect of stepping into that stark room and seeing his carriage surrounded by thick burgundy ropes was powerful. The damage done by the bombs that killed him had not been repaired, for effect we assumed; a door hung from its hinges, the carriage wheels were askew, spokes were missing, there was smoke damage on the wood.

Vera and I walked through the room looking at the pictures, reading the notes and newspaper articles hanging on the walls in slim black frames. The carriage had been a gift from Emperor Napoleon III of France we learned. It was supposed to be bomb-proof. Five Cossacks had been in the carriage with Alexander. The chief of police and the chief of the emperor's guards followed closely in separate sleighs.

There were pictures of horses rearing and people running with their arms over their heads and their mouths open. There was even one of Alexander bending over his carriage inspecting the damage from the first bomb just before the second bomb, the one that ripped his legs off below the knees, exploded. He died a few hours later at the Winter Palace.

His son, Alexander III, took power immediately, claimed his father's murder was a Jewish plot, and reversed all the reforms his father had made to create a more liberal, inclusive empire. Jews were once again prohibited from living, working, or owning land outside prescribed boundaries. We were forbidden from working in the civil service, from attending universities, from doing business on Christian holidays. The word *pogrom* became part of the English language.

* * *

Vera and I went to the Russian Tea Room after the exhibit, but there was such a lineup, we decided to catch the Number 7 home instead. The El was surprisingly crowded for a Monday afternoon so we stood, our fingers wrapped around the overhead straps as the train snaked through the tunnels.

"If he hadn't been killed," Vera said, "we might still be living in Russia. Amazing isn't it, how one event can change so many lives."

"We saw him in St. Petersburg, the tsar. Pappa took us."

"Really? What do you remember?"

"Not much. I was so young. I remember Pappa hoisting me up on his shoulders so I could see. He was on a balcony at the Winter Palace with his family. They waved at us. Mostly I remember their big red dog. He had a long feathery tail."

Vera chuckled as we swayed companionably, bracing our legs as the train swerved.

"Did Esther's train leave on time yesterday?" Vera asked.

"Yes. She was looking forward to going home, I think."

"Given what you've told me about Winnipeg, I can't imagine why."

"She seems to like it. She always did. I gave her Margaret's latest book for the trip home. She was flipping through it a few days ago and I thought she might find it interesting."

"Esther reading Margaret Sanger? Don't you think Margaret's a little radical for Esther?"

"Not really. She does have an inquisitive side."

The El veered sharply and I almost fell into two old women sitting in the seats in front of us. They were probably not much older than Vera and me, but in their black babushkas with the pink roses, they could have been from another century.

"I don't know why you worry about her so much," one said to the other. "It doesn't help."

"It does help," the other answered testily. "If you worry about something, it won't happen. It's only when you stop worrying that you've got something to worry about."

Vera put her hand on my shoulder. "You're worrying about her, aren't you?"

"I am. When I asked her to come to the exhibit, I thought for a moment she was going into one of the altered states the psychiatrist told me about when she was with me for those two years."

"That was twenty years ago, Anna," Vera said. "She seemed fine."

"Maybe she was fine. Maybe she wasn't. Esther can always appear to be fine. I seem to be the only one who knows when she isn't."

* * *

Two days later, I wake up freezing. Listening for the hum of the furnace and cursing Jake for not delivering the coal again, I try the light switch. Nothing. I pull on socks and a wool robe and feel my way down the stairs to my office to see if the whole city is out or just my house. Blackouts aren't a nightly event but the military has been cutting the electricity with no warning when they fear German bombers might appear overhead.

I hear footsteps coming up the stairs to my apartment then and a quick knock on the door. "Anna," Vera whispers, "are you up? We don't have lights or heat downstairs."

As if on cue, Jake's shovel starts scraping in the basement, the lights come on, and the telephone rings. We laugh through the door. Vera pads back downstairs and I go to my desk to answer the phone.

"May I speak with Bencke Grieve please?"

I'm confused. Nobody but Esther calls me Bencke.

"I'm sorry to be calling so early, Miss Grieve. My name is Inspector Lee McHugh. I'm with the Winnipeg Police Services."

My body stiffens. This isn't the first time the Winnipeg police have called me about Esther.

"Do you know an Esther Kinnear?" he asks.

"Yes. Esther Kinnear is my sister."

"I'm afraid I have some bad news, Miss Grieve. Your sister's been in an accident."

"An accident? What happened?"

"I think it might be better to talk about this in person."

I'm already in flight; making a reservation, packing, canceling my hair appointment. "Is she all right?"

"I'm afraid not, Miss Grieve. She's dead."

"Dead? She can't be. She was just here."

"We can discuss this in more detail when you're here. Do you know where the Ness Street Station is?"

I do. It's the station I went to the last time the police called.

I'm scarcely aware of hanging up the phone. The room seems to be in a state of suspension. The sofa, the coffee table, my magazines and newspapers, all seem to be waiting for me to do something but I'm not sure what it is I'm supposed to do, what it is I ever did at this time of day.

Maybe it's not Esther, I think suddenly, and call her home in Winnipeg.

Her maid answers after eight rings. "Kinnear residence."

15

"Is she there, Louise?"

She doesn't recognize my voice.

"It's Anna Grieve. Esther's sister from Manhattan."

She hesitates. "Didn't the police call you?"

"They did. Do you know what happened?"

"No. They told Branson and me that Mrs. Kinnear had an unfortunate accident and said we should find alternate accommodations until we hear from them. I was packing when you called. My sister in St. Boniface says I can move in with her. Do you know when Mrs. Kinnear will be back?"

Unexpectedly, as always, the pain cuts through my temple like a dagger as I'm saying good-bye. The doctors told me stress could bring it on.

I walk to the kitchen for a coffee but my hands are shaking so badly it's hard to keep the kettle still enough to fill. I turn and reach for a cup. When I turn back for the boiling water, I can't see the kettle anywhere.

The top of my forehead throbbing now, I walk back to the window in my office. Esther had stood here with me a few days ago, a coffee cup in one hand, rubbing her eyes with the other. "Why do you get up so early, Bencke?" she asked me sleepily.

"To see this," I said, motioning to the pink and purple streaks in the sky, the gold haloes outlining the clouds and high rises.

"Mmm," she said, steam from her coffee drifting up her face. "It *is* beautiful. I love this coffee. I've got to switch to instant when I get home. What kind is this?"

She asked me that question again when I took her to the station to go back to Winnipeg. Turning to me from the vestibule stairs, she smiled down at me. "What kind of coffee did you say you buy?"

"Nescafé," I called up to her.

Those were our last words.

Looking down from my office window now, the pain settled firmly behind my left eye, I watch Earl, the bouncer from the brothel a few doors away as he shines a flashlight up and down a light standard. A cabbie beside him nods his head in agreement with whatever Earl is saying. I'll have to ask him to look after my car while I'm gone; I'll have to find someone to give my lecture at the women's shelter.

I slide down the wall and sit beneath the window, bringing my knees close to my chest, remembering how often I used to sit just like this outside Esther's bedroom door in Winnipeg.

* * *

The tears start when I'm on the train to Winnipeg and realize I'm seeing the same things Esther must have seen on her way home a few days ago. They fill my eyes and spill down my face, salty and cool as they slide under the neck of my blouse.

"Coffee, Miss?"

"Shoeshine, Miss?"

"The dining car is open for lunch, Miss."

The attendant doesn't seem to find it unusual that a full-grown woman is sitting in her seat doing nothing to stop herself from crying.

A young woman with a small boy in tow stops in front of me. She's compact with dark curly hair, her boy a carbon copy. "Would you like this, Miss?" she asks, holding a box of tissues out to me. It makes the tears come faster.

I sleep in snatches and wake to images that disappear as I apprehend them: my mother's face the last time I saw her from the window of the train that took Esther and me away from Russia; flakes of green paint peeling from a hospital ceiling as I'm rushed along on a gurney, my stomach so distended I can't see past it.

17

"Coffee, Miss?"

"Next stop Minneapolis, Miss."

"The dining car is open for dinner, Miss."

When I go to the washroom I'm shocked to see that I look the same. Nothing is the same now that Esther is dead. I wash with the harsh yellow soap and rough paper towels and go back to my seat with my skin burning, a momentary and welcome diversion to the heartache and nausea that are traveling with me.

"Coffee, Miss?"

"Newspaper?"

I take the *Winnipeg Free Press*.

News about the war, but mostly local stories: Ottawa has recalled pleasure vehicles bought in Manitoba between December of last year and February 15 to have their tires retreaded; a rail boxcar has been discovered on an abandoned farm in Carmen, Manitoba, filled with what paleontologists think are the remains of buffalo bones.

An editorial on page three discusses the ethical aspects of an event that took place in Winnipeg a few days earlier—a simulated Nazi invasion staged by the Victory Bonds Committee to raise money for the war effort. If Day, it was called, as in what-if-it-happened-here. The editorial says that although the exercise was for a good cause, it was in bad taste and potentially frightening for anyone who didn't know it was simulated. The words become a blur. I slide the newspaper under my seat.

* * *

It's dusk when the taxi lets me off in front of the Ness Street station. It's exactly as I remembered it: a one-story brick building on the outskirts of a run-down residential area in the north end. Identical bungalows are cheek-on-jowl along the sidewalks, and icy gray snow is piled high on the curbs. Nathaniel and I used to climb over icy mounds like this when we were young, our mittened hands to our throats, croaking "Water, water," pretending we were lost in the desert.

When I give the duty officer my name, he picks up the phone immediately and moments later, the inspector comes down the hall toward me, tightening his tie. His loose gait and long arms remind me of Nathaniel. I hope I don't run into him while I'm here.

"How was your trip?" the inspector asks when we're seated in his office, sliding a file folder on his desk closer.

"Uneventful."

"Can I get you a coffee, or something a little stronger?" His hand goes to a desk drawer.

"No thank you."

"Are you up to answering a few questions?"

"Yes."

"You live in Manhattan."

"Yes."

"How long have you lived there?"

"Forty-eight years."

"Before that you lived in Winnipeg?"

"Yes." My voice sounds to me like it's coming from very far away.

"Did your sister live in Manhattan with you, Miss Grieve?"

"She did for a few years, but that was twenty years ago."

"And she was visiting you just now?"

"How do you know that?"

He looks up at me, his finger on a white hand-written page. "We found train tickets in her purse."

"Yes. She was visiting for a week."

"Was she under any stress?"

"No. She was lovely."

19

* * *

She *was* lovely. She'd put on a few pounds and it suited her so well. Except for not wanting to see the exhibit on Alexander II, she was up for everything, *Porgy and Bess* at the Alvin, art galleries, and shopping. She tried on a black feather tilt in the hat department at Saks and paraded around with her cheeks sucked in and her hips jutting out like a model. We laughed and the saleslady laughed with us and told us what good friends we were.

"Oh, we're not friends," Esther said. "We're sisters."

The saleslady was surprised and so was I. It was so unlike Esther to reveal anything about herself. "I never would have guessed," the saleslady said. "You look so different."

We did look different. Well past middle age, I'm still six feet tall with an athletic build and a dark chin-length bob that I keep sleek with a lifetime supply of Brylcreem. Esther was my polar opposite: blond, small, alabaster skin, bird-like bones. Everyone assumed she was the younger.

After Saks we went to Childs and had the chicken salad. Esther said it was better at the Grill Room in Winnipeg and laughed and reached out for my hand. "It's nice to have something that's better in Winnipeg, Bencke," she said and then, "Let's not allow so much time to pass before next time."

I was tempted then to ask her whether the attacks had stopped but I didn't. We had stopped discussing them so many years ago and I didn't want to ruin her equanimity, or mine.

* * *

"Miss Grieve," the inspector says, interrupting my reverie, "would you rather continue in the morning?"

"No, thank you. I'm fine. Why do you ask if she was under any stress?"

Hesitating carefully, he says, "Because it looks like suicide."

I fight to keep the nausea down. "What exactly happened, Inspector? You've only told me there was an accident."

"Two witnesses say they saw your sister walk into the path of an oncoming train."

"I'm confused. This accident happened at the train station?"

"Yes. Your sister's train from Manhattan had just arrived. The witnesses say she got off her train and walked directly onto the track at the other side of the station. A train was coming through with coal for the armament smelters in the east. They don't stop here."

"Couldn't she have tripped or been pushed?"

"That's a fair question, Miss Grieve. Do you know if she had any enemies, if anyone was harassing her?"

I only know what Esther has been telling me. For years that's been positive.

"We'll be checking all possibilities. Department protocol is to treat every death as suspicious until proven otherwise. There will be a report from the coroner and we'll interview her staff, looking for a suicide note, a threatening letter, anything that can shed light on what happened. But. . ." he flips back a few pages in his folder ". . . this incident with the baby does suggest mental instability."

This incident with the baby.

"That was twenty-two years ago, Inspector." I thought I had cried myself dry on the train but my eyes start to fill again. "Are you even sure it's Esther? May I see the body?"

21

"The body is in the morgue, Miss Grieve. It's closed. Why don't we finish here and get you to your hotel?"

"Inspector," I say, my voice breaking, "I've been sitting in a coach listening to a toothpick click against the teeth of the man beside me for three and a half days because you asked me to get here as soon as possible. My only living relative in the world is dead and now you tell me that I can't even see if it's her?"

"I'm sorry, Miss Grieve," he says and closes the file. "I don't have a key. Nobody in the police station does. The morgue is in a hospital on Taché Avenue and it's closed until morning."

I look up and try to breathe deeply. There's a Saks hatbox and what looks like one of Esther's journals on a credenza to the left of his desk.

"Are those Esther's?" I ask.

"Yes."

"May I have them?"

"Not until the investigation is over," he says, walking to the door. "It's late. Let me drive you to your hotel. I'll pick you up tomorrow morning at five-thirty so we can be at the hospital when the morgue opens at six."

"Please let me take her journal to the hotel."

"I can't do that, Miss Grieve. It's not policy."

"Have you read it?"

"Yes."

"Is there any indication of why she did this?"

"Not that I could see."

"Would you be willing to let me look? She's been keeping journals since she was a girl. I read a few early on. If there was a clue in this one, I might recognize it before you would. I'll give it back to you in the morning."

"I'm sorry, Miss Grieve," he says, shaking his head. "I'd like to help you, but I can't."

He takes his parka from a coat hook and holds the door open for me. We drive to the Fort Garry Hotel in silence.

"Would you like me to come in with you?" he asks when we get there.

"No thank you, Inspector. I'll see you in the morning."

* * *

Pulling back the accordion gate when we reach the elevator, the bellhop looks at me proudly. "We're getting automatic elevator doors soon," he says. "Make it much easier with luggage and all, although some of our guests will be sorry to see these go."

We get off at the second floor. "This way, Ma'am." He stops in front of Room 204.

It's a small room, grays and mauves with just enough space for the high brass bed, a luggage rack at the foot of the bed, and a tall Victorian wardrobe beside the bed that opens out into a desk. The bellhop puts my case on the luggage rack. Stomach rumbling, I give him a tip and call room service for a toasted club sandwich and a scotch. I hadn't eaten anything except peanuts and coffee on the train. I ask the operator to make sure they don't knock, to leave the cart outside the door in about twenty minutes.

I'm manipulating the copper bathtub taps with my toes when the knocking starts. It sounds like it's coming from the other side of the bathroom wall, not the door. I wonder if it's the ghosts I read about years earlier. Apparently a woman hung herself in the closet in the room next to mine after her husband died in a car accident. Guests who had stayed in that room since said they heard strange knocking in the night.

Another knock, more insistent this time. I step out of the tub, wrap myself in my robe, and go to the door. There's a large brown envelope leaning against the wall. I pull out Esther's journal, surprised and not surprised that Inspector McHugh has gone to the trouble. I'd sensed some compassion at the police station.

There's only one entry. It's dated February 18, the day after she left Manhattan.

The storm in Minneapolis held us up for about an hour and I was glad to have the book that Bencke gave me. My compartment is fine and clean and the bunk seems comfortable. It's snowing softly outside. The little farmhouses in the distance look so safe. It was a wonderful visit. Bencke was in top form as usual and a perfect hostess although I could tell she was looking forward to getting back to her own life. It was good to see Vera again and to meet her friend Ben. They seem very happy together. I'm sorry I didn't tell Bencke my good news. I will tell her soon. She'll be happy for me. I think I'll pick up Licorice from the kennel before I go home. I am excited to see my little sidekick.

I flip through the rest of the journal. Nothing. I turn it upside down and shake it to see if anything will fall out. Nothing. I wonder what her good news was. Whatever it was, it's clear that she wasn't suicidal. You don't wax poetic about snow and look forward to seeing your dog if you're planning to kill yourself.

I walk to the window and look down over the city. It's dark and deserted, streetlights illuminating the crystals of ice hanging from the bare branches of the trees in the park across the street. All so familiar.

The shop on William Street where Esther and I went as teenagers to have our fortunes told has been torn down and replaced by a four-story office building with a black metal fire escape snaking down one side. It was a hat shop when Esther and I went there; J. Farkas Hatter to Gentlemen, etched in a semicircle in a large, loopy script on the front pane. A white hand-lettered sign leaned into the left bottom corner of the window: "Mrs. Eva Farkas. Professional Seer. Recently arrived from Europe. Never a wrong answer in love or business or health for over twenty years."

Esther hadn't wanted to have her fortune told. She was afraid of what the fortune-teller would say, afraid of going to that part of town, afraid the Count and Countess would find out, but I pushed her and she agreed.

A bell on the door dinged and a man in his shirtsleeves stopped dusting the hats on a shelf and gave us the once-over. "She's in back," he said dryly. We were no novelty, I gathered.

The curtain opened on a large humid room with two women in it. One had her broad back to us, her sleeves rolled up over muscular arms. She was stirring something sharp-smelling in a pot on a small black stove. The other woman was facing us, seated at a sewing machine, her feet moving rapidly on the treadle. She stopped and gave us a mocking smile.

She was the same age as the Countess I guessed, but so different, with her wiry red hair escaping from its combs and her bosoms pillowing out over her tight lavender blouse.

"You want to know about love, yes?" she asked, pushing her chair back and walking to a small round table covered with a red fringed cloth at the back of the shop. "Come. Sit. Take off gloves, hats. Is hot in here. How you get my name, young ladies?"

"I can't remember," I lied. I was reluctant to tell her that Agnes, the Countess's seamstress, had told me about her.

"I do leaves, cards, palms, all fifteen cents," she said, the smile never leaving her face. "If you like, I guess names too and ages for ten cents more. What you want?"

"Just tea leaves, please."

She turned to Esther. "And you, Miss?"

"The same, please."

"The same please, of course." She went to the stove and came back to the table with two cups of steaming dark tea. "Don't touch," she said, sitting down at the table. "Let tea sit." She put her elbows on the table and her chin in her hands and smiled while we waited.

It was a wonderful room. Hat forms were lined up, small to large, on shelves along one wall. Squares of felt in browns and grays and blacks were stacked above them. Rolls of grosgrain ribbons in the same colors were looped over hooks in the opposite wall. And there were giant spools of thread on that wall, each one sticking out from a nail in the wall.

I remember wondering why Agnes didn't set up a system like this at home. She spent so much time going through her sewing basket to find just the right thread for the Countess's gowns and tea clothes and walking suits.

"Drink now," Mrs. Farkas said. "Leave little bit in bottom, then pick up cup with right hand."

We did what she said.

"Now move cup in circle to left three times. Good. Now to right three times. Good. Now put cup upside down in saucer and slide to me. Don't shake. Slide, dears."

She looked into my cup and tipped it toward me. "You see bear here?" she said, drawing a ragged red fingernail over what looked to me like a blob of tea leaves. "Means travel. And this," she said, excited now, tracing a sparse, broken line of leaves, "means big decisions coming for such a young woman. I see money, romance, an older man with name M or N."

The smile left her face when she picked up Esther's cup. "Maybe you come back another day. I charge you today only for one reading."

* * *

A rattling in the hall stops at my door. Just the thought of food makes me salivate. I wait a few moments and wheel the cart in and bite into the sweet, salty, crunchy sandwich faster than I can swallow. When it's gone, I lick my index finger and lift the crumbs of bread and bacon that have fallen on the plate to my mouth. I take the cut-glass tumbler of scotch to the bed.

I have the dream again that night, the dream that I know now is as much fact as fantasy. It always starts the same way. I'm about five years old, in the root cellar of our one-room home in Russia. It's cold and dark and the ceiling is so low I can touch it if I put my hands up. I don't though. There are spiders on the ceiling that crawl down your arms if you do. I stand there, my arms tight at my sides, looking up at the stairs. I'm waiting for someone to come down and get me, afraid to go up. Mamma has told me if I make any noise when I'm in the cellar bad men will take me away. Suddenly there are boots stomping above me. Men's loud voices. Esther starts screaming and then Mamma. I put my hands over my ears and close my eyes. When I open them, my arms have grown wings, sheer white wings with fluted edges and fine white veins. I'm not afraid anymore. I lift my wings and fly through the cellar door and lift Esther in my arms and we soar through the roof and into the sky. Sometimes Pappa is with us, his wings white as well, larger than mine, and we all three soar together, banking and smiling softly at each other when our eyes meet.

27

I wake up just after midnight, soaking wet and freezing and take a long hot shower, letting the water pound my face and stream over my hair. I call room service then for black tea with honey and toast. I pull the desk chair to the window, take the gray tapestry spread from the bed and wrap it around my shoulders and sit at the window with Esther's journal on my lap, waiting for morning.

• CHAPTER THREE •

"I hope I didn't wake you with my knocking," Inspector McHugh says when I slide into the car beside him the next morning and give him the journal.

"You didn't," I say, wondering what prompted his change of heart. "Thank you for bringing it to the hotel last night."

"I'm sorry I didn't let you take it at the station yesterday," he says, dropping the journal into an open black briefcase on the floor behind his seat. "I was being a bit of a stickler. Did you find anything of interest?"

"No, there was just the one entry, as you know. I don't think she was suicidal."

"It didn't look like it to me either." He reaches forward to put the key in the ignition and turns to me. "Didn't you bring anything warmer?"

I'm shivering in the same gray suit and gray suede shoes I had on yesterday at the police station. I haven't brought anything warmer. "I wasn't thinking clearly when I packed."

"When are you going back to Manhattan?"

"I'm not sure. I have to see the lawyer and make arrangements about the house and the funeral."

"Then we better get you some warm clothes. If you have the time, I can take you to a factory in St. Vital that makes the parkas for the force. They're down-filled with wolf trim hoods. Very warm."

I wonder again why he's being so nice to me. "They let civilians walk around in police-issue parkas?" I ask.

He laughs. "No. They make private-label outdoor gear for construction companies and city employees too, that kind of thing. They're not available through retail outlets."

Except for a garbage truck groaning along the curb, the street is empty. Pools of yellow glow from the overhead light standards illuminating the patches of black ice; Inspector McHugh glides over them expertly. I move my feet closer to the warm air register and settle in.

Ten minutes later, the hospital comes as a shock. It's the same one I found Esther in after what Inspector McHugh referred to yesterday as "this incident with the baby." He drives to the parking lot at the back. There's a bay window on the second floor that looks like the one in the room I found Esther in that day. I had thought then that things couldn't get much worse.

The inspector nods to people as we walk along the hall. He seems to know everybody—the orderlies, the cleaning staff, the doctors and nurses, even some of the patients. He stops at Room 106 and pushes the door open for me.

A man in a white jacket is standing beside a table covered with a white sheet. When he sees us, he pulls the sheet back. Having become very good over the years at putting Esther out of my mind, I haven't allowed myself to think this far ahead. When I see her face, I gag and run out of the room.

Inspector McHugh is at the door when I come out of the washroom. "I'm sorry," I say, the taste of bile bitter in my mouth.

"Please don't be. It's not a pleasant thing to see." He takes a form out of his briefcase and gestures to a wooden bench. "Let's sit there for a moment. I need to hear you say your sister's name and have you sign this form.

* * *

"Did the train run over her?" I ask on the way back to the hotel.

"No. The train was going very fast. It threw her into the air. She landed on a monument beside the station."

I try not to imagine the scene, to keep the image of her at the morgue out of my mind and concentrate on the street around me. It's still early, but the city is coming to life. People are brushing snow from their windshields. A little boy with red mitts is wailing as his mother pulls him along behind her. Small groups of women are walking together, laughing. On their way to wartime jobs I imagine. I wonder how long it will be until everyday life starts to matter to me again.

"Is there anyone I can call for you?" the inspector asks when we pull up at the hotel. "A relative, a friend?"

"There's no one."

He's quiet for a few moments. "If you're up to it, I can have an officer meet you at your sister's house at two tomorrow afternoon. It's not procedure, but I thought you might want to look around before the police team goes through. We'll be restricting access to the property at that point."

"Why will you be restricting access?" I ask.

"We might find evidence that sheds some light on what she did or why, perhaps another slant on her death. We don't want anyone going in until the investigation is over."

"I'd like very much to go there tomorrow, then. Thank you."

* * *

I'm surprised and pleased when Inspector McHugh answers Esther's door the next day.

"I got out of a meeting early," he says, "and thought it would be easier for you this way."

It's all so familiar. The cream-colored wainscoting, the large brass umbrella stand, even the smell—Esther's perfume mingled with lemon furniture polish and the smell of Licorice.

I realize suddenly that I don't know where the dog is. "Where's Licorice?"

"He's still at the kennel I believe. We'll have to find him a permanent home, unless you want to take him back with you. Look around, Miss Grieve. We have about two hours."

"Can I open drawers and closets?"

"I'm going to sit right here and read this newspaper. You can do whatever you want. Just don't take anything."

It feels strange to be here without Esther. The magazines in her study are neatly stacked on a side table. The porcelain angels she collects are lined up on a windowsill as if they're on a walking pilgrimage. I expect her to show up at any moment, Licorice clicking along at her heels.

I open the middle drawer of her small oval desk. It's neat and orderly. There's a daybook with notes for appointments and luncheons, a tortoiseshell comb, a monogrammed handkerchief, pens, and, under it all, what feels like a journal. I glance at the doorway to make sure the inspector isn't looking and take it out. It starts on March 4, 1888.

Inspector McHugh coughs and I panic. I don't want him to know I've found the journal but I have no place to hide it. I almost laugh out loud when I figure out what to do. Taking my suit jacket off and laying it across Esther's desk, I undo the button on my skirt, and pull the zipper down. I pull my blouse out, bend forward, and, keeping my eyes on the doorway, place the journal on my back. I secure one end under my brassiere band and the other under the waist of my girdle. I stand up and wiggle around a bit around to make sure it won't fall out, then put my clothes back on and walk, very erectly, back into the hall.

Inspector McHugh looks at his watch and then up at me. "There's plenty of time left, Miss Grieve."

"I can't do this right now. I feel like I'm invading her privacy."

"I understand." He looks at his watch again. "Have you had lunch?"

"No, I haven't."

"Would you like to join me?"

I'm surprised to find that I would. I'm comfortable with this man. I decide the journal can wait. From what I remember, 1888 was a good year for Esther. I'll have lunch and read the journal later. It will be nice to go over some of the good times in her life. I ask the inspector to stop at the hotel, run up the stairs to my room and take the journal out of my underwear.

***

"I'm surprised you don't know about this place," Inspector McHugh says as we slide into a red faux leather booth at a Salisbury House. "It's a chain started by an American actor down on his luck. Good basic food. Hamburgers—they call them nips—omelettes and pancakes, great coffee, and bran muffins. One of our recruits brings a dozen to the station every Friday morning and they're gone by ten. No one is ever seen eating one and no one admits to it. We call it the bran muffin mysteries."

I laugh. "How long have these restaurants been around?" I ask.

"Since the Depression."

33

"Well, that explains it. I haven't been back since then."

The waitress comes over to fill our coffee cups and I watch the inspector following the steaming brown liquid as it fills his cup. He's appealing in a heavy-featured kind of way, square face, pock-marked cheeks, full lips, salt-and-pepper hair that needs a trim. He looks up at me. His eyes are brown and warm. I wonder how you keep your humanity in a job like his.

"Were you born here?" I ask when the waitress has left. "I sometimes think I hear a hint of an English accent in your voice."

"You have a good ear. I was born in England. We came over when I was seven."

"You have family? Children?"

"No. To both questions. My wife died about five years ago in much the same circumstances as your sister."

"You mean suicide?"

"Yes."

"I'm sorry to hear that, Inspector. Does that mean you're convinced that Esther's death was a suicide?"

"There's no evidence to suggest otherwise."

"Yet."

He smiles at me. "Yes, yet. We still have a few things to look into."

"How long do you think that will take?"

"No more than a week. How about you? Were you born in Winnipeg?"

"No. Esther and I were born in a small town in Russia called Podensk. You won't find it on a map. I don't know if it even exists anymore. It was inland, between St. Petersburg and Moscow.

"Ah, so the name Bencke is Russian. I wondered. I've never heard that name before."

I chuckle. "My name is Anna. Bencke is my nickname. It's from a Yiddish word. Until I was a year old, I cried whenever they took me out of the house. They said I was bencken. That's homesick in Yiddish."

• CHAPTER FOUR •

When he's paid the bill, Inspector McHugh suggests we go to the clothing factory. "It's only about fifteen minutes away. Do you have time?"

I do. I'm chilled right through, and Esther's journal will be waiting when I get back to the hotel.

The factory is in an industrial area on the outskirts of the city. It's a low cream-colored stucco building with a flat roof, divided into side-by-side units, their names printed in white on a black strip that runs under the roofline: Mazak Glove and Safety, Latem Plastics, St. Jacob Signs, and at the end Diamond Head Work Wear.

We walk into a showroom, which has a high round pedestal in the center with a black phone perched on top. Behind it, clothes are hanging on metal racks with boots and accessories in glass units against the walls. Everything looks to me like variations on a theme. Shapeless waterproof parkas in beige or black, hip length or mid-thigh, wolf trim around the hood or no trim, lined pants to match with elastic waists.

I choose beige, mid-thigh, no trim, black boots, and sheepskin mitts. Inspector McHugh places the order at the telephone and a few moments later, a man in a gray smock comes into the showroom with a big cardboard box. Thirty-five dollars for a parka and pants, gloves, and boots. He puts the box in the backseat of the car.

On the way back to the hotel, the car stalls in front of a vacant lot on Main Street that's littered with old tires and appliances.

"Sorry," Inspector McHugh says. "Needs a bit of a rest. Do you mind if we sit here for a few moments?" He reaches into the backseat. "Would you like to put on your parka?"

"We'll be at the hotel soon," I say. "Let's not bother." I tuck my fingers under my armpits, flashing back to our early days in Winnipeg; to white rabbit muffs and pottery bed warmers, to cashmere chemises and drawers and socks imported from England, none of it up to a Winnipeg winter. I still get chilblains when the weather is below zero. Esther did too.

"Didn't there used to be a shoe store here?" I ask.

"Yes. Thomas Regan Boots and Shoes. It burned down nine or ten years ago. They made the boots for the military. Made these, in fact," he says, lifting a shiny black lace-up.

"They made our shoes too. Nothing like the shoes you're wearing or the shoes we had made for us in Italy."

"You had your shoes made in Italy?" He sounds incredulous.

"We did. Two or three times a year we would go down to the kitchen and Davis, one of our footmen, would trace our feet on brown paper and send the tracings to some place in Italy. For the longest time I thought that was his job."

"His job?"

"Footman. Tracing feet."

He throws his head back and laughs, a full, explosive sound that seems to surprise him as much as my joke did.

"After we'd been here for three or four years, the Count decided we should start shopping locally."

"The Count?" he asks.

"Yes. Count and Countess Chernovski. They brought us to Winnipeg from Russia. They were our guardians."

I can see him searching his mind. "Yes," he said. "The Count was in lumber if I remember correctly and the Countess was responsible for the Ellis Street Sanctuary for unwed mothers."

"Yes. That's right. Esther volunteered at the Sanctuary too."

"And you all had your shoes made in Italy?" He can't get over it.

"We did. About fourteen weeks after we sent the drawings of our feet to Italy, a box filled with the most beautiful shoes would arrive. Completely inappropriate for Winnipeg. Suede shoes with leather trim, ankle-high calfskin boots with silk laces. It's one of the fond memories I have of growing up here."

* * *

There were days, sometimes weeks, when life in our palatial home in Armstrong's Point was predictable, even peaceful. Esther had her piano and a group of neighborhood girlfriends. The Count was deeply and happily involved with the lumberyards his cousin had convinced him to buy into. They could barely keep up with the demand for the fir and cedar they were importing from British Columbia.

The Countess was busy with the house, her charity work, our upbringing and education. We studied English literature and spoken French, Russian, and Italian. We had a penmanship tutor and a classically trained French ballet teacher who came in twice a week to teach us deportment. Esther studied piano and I took voice for a few months.

But our relationship, the Countess's and mine, was never easy. I believed for the longest time that she was responsible for taking us

away from Mamma and couldn't forgive her. She resented me as well,
I think now not only because of how difficult I was, but because of the
friction I suspect I caused between her and the Count. The only disagreement I heard them have was about me, but over the years, there
must have been more.

* * *

The disagreement I overheard took place on the steamer from Le Havre
to Halifax a few days after we boarded. Esther and I were in bunk
beds on one side of the cabin with the heavy velvet curtain pulled. The
Count and Countess were on the other side, their curtain pulled as
well. The Countess was speaking more loudly than she usually did, so
I caught her tone of voice if nothing else. She was clearly upset about
what he was telling her.

After breakfast the next morning, the Count left our cabin for a
few minutes and returned with a roll of soft white twine. He took out
his pearl-handled pocketknife, told me to stand still and straight, and
went to work. He cut two lengths of twine to fit over my shoulders
like suspenders, tied them to a third length that went around my waist
and tied a fourth length at the back for a leash. He fastened it on me
whenever we left our private rooms for the rest of the trip.

By the time we got to Winnipeg, the harness was my favorite game.
The Countess's disapproval when I wore it was palpable. She never said
anything directly, but I never heard her say anything directly. She just
arranged her face into that tense, smiling mask that I came to know
so well over the years and excused herself from whatever room I was
barking and wagging my way through.

* * *

39

In all the years I lived with her, I can only remember three occasions when I knew what the Countess was feeling.

The first time was the day we arrived in Winnipeg. The train slowed and jerked, the sound of the whistle muffled by the howling of the wind outside. Even in our closed compartment, it sounded fierce.

"We're here," the Count said excitedly and started scraping the frost off the window, little bits of it clinging to his knife.

The Countess joined him, put her hand on his back, and peered out the small area he had cleared. She gasped then and ran out of the compartment. The Count followed, leaving the flimsy door flapping open behind him.

After a few moments, Esther and I approached the window, afraid of what we were going to see. A full-scale blizzard was underway, the wind driving the snow horizontally, almost obliterating the row of long unpainted immigration sheds across from the station. The few people we saw outside were holding on to each other to remain upright.

After what seemed like a lifetime although it was probably only a few moments, the Count and Countess came back. He had his arm around her shoulders. She was leaning on him and her eyes were red. A train attendant followed behind them. The Count asked us to go with the attendant—that he was going to show us the engine. We followed, pretending that we were interested in what he was showing us when we got there, terrified that we were now going to be abandoned by the Count and Countess as well as our parents.

Years later, Esther told me that the Countess thought that Winnipeg looked like Siberia. She had known of course that she was moving to a place called the Wild West and was looking forward to the adventure, but for some reason, she thought Winnipeg would be like the small towns she knew in Europe, that it would have cobbled streets and fine shops and medieval churches.

Winnipeg's streets were not cobbled; they were dirt. In summer, the dirt turned to dust and coated your nostrils. In winter it turned to black ice. The shops were not fine; they were primitive; there was a moneylender, a saddlery, several dry goods establishments. The only thing medieval about the city was the torture of the mosquitoes in the summers and the cold in the winters.

There were a few fine residential areas like the one we were to live in and a smattering of ornate European-style buildings and churches in the downtown area, but by and large, the city was bleak.

The population at that time and for years afterwards was mainly single transient men. Standing like statues on hotel verandas with cigarettes hanging from their lips and blankets around their shoulders, the very sight of them frightened the Countess. At first, we never went out without one of our strongest footmen along. But she found out soon enough, we all did, that these men had little interest in immigrants, rich or poor. They were traveling with the railway, laying tracks. They made a good wage and found more than enough distraction in the local brothels and hastily erected theaters that featured "exotic" talent.

When I started wandering around the city with Nathaniel, we saw posters advertising this talent, all of it brought in from the United States: a sharpshooter who demonstrated his skills from a trapeze, a one-legged woman who danced on sand, a man who could shatter wine glasses with his falsetto.

* * *

I saw the Countess's vulnerability again when the Count's library furniture arrived from Podensk. Her furniture had been arriving for months, the library furniture, the last batch.

41

She hovered and fretted and pointed this way and that as the burly men carried the Count's desk and chair and side tables and loveseat into the library. She had them try things here and there and when she was finally satisfied and let the men go, she brushed away invisible dust, smoothed antimacassars on the chairs, repositioned side tables.

When the Count came home that evening, she took him straight to his library, Esther and I following behind them.

His face lit up when he entered the room. Sitting down in his big leather chair, he ran his hand over his desk and smiled up at her. "Wonderful," he said. "What a wonderful job you've done, my dear. It feels like home, doesn't it?"

Her face broke up. She turned abruptly and left the room.

With the house in order, she started entertaining. I remember the first dinner party well because it was the only time it felt like we were a family. The Countess had taught the cook to make the Count's favorite dessert, *chak-chak*, and was very excited about it. It was to be a surprise, she told Esther and me almost gaily, and we must keep it a secret. She let us stay up late to watch the dinner party from the window of a small anteroom off the dining room where the food was placed before it was served. "You must be quiet," she told us, "and you must not touch the food." She actually patted me on the shoulder and smiled when she said that.

The dining room was beautiful: sixteen white orchids in white porcelain pots lined up precisely along the center of the dining room table; twenty white tapers glowing in the wrought iron candelabra that had been lowered for the occasion. The women sparkled. The men's voices were deep and resonant.

The chak-chak, a pile of glistening egg noodles drizzled with honey, sat on a large white platter on a table behind us. When none of the servants were around, I'd been moving back to break off the little crusty bits at the ends. They were delicious.

After the main course dishes had been cleared away, a footman sailed in from behind us and went to lift the platter. I was stepping back for another crusty bit at that moment and he tripped over my foot, sending the platter flying. Esther and the footman and I watched the chak-chak slide back and forth in slow motion, then explode in a shiny, gooey mess on the floor, the dish following, shattering loudly. The Countess rushed in to the anteroom and burst into tears. So did I.

Getting on my hands and knees to try to pick up the pieces, my voice trembling, I apologized. "Maybe Joseph can fix it," I said, picking up one of the largest pieces of the platter and turning to her. But she wasn't in the room anymore.

• CHAPTER FIVE •

I'm surprised to see that it's almost five when Inspector McHugh and I get back to the hotel with my box of clothes. I'm even more surprised that I haven't thought about Esther for most of the afternoon. The bellhop takes the box from the car to the elevator. I can barely wait to read the journal that's waiting for me.

Esther was sixteen in 1888 and, in my twelve-year-old eyes, perfect. She was petite and beautiful with tiny feet and long, slender hands. Her skin was milky white and glowed. Her eyelashes, despite her fairness, were dark and long, making her light blue eyes even more startling. And she was elegant. She could laugh and smile without showing her teeth. Nobody, myself included, could keep their eyes from her.

She was also kind. She tried to include me in her social circle, inviting me on sleigh rides with her friends and to croquet parties and teas, and church socials, but it never worked. I knew from sneaking into her room and reading her journals that her friends made fun of my awkwardness, my height, my large hands and feet. They lurched around the room with a hand over one eye, miming my awkward gait and the eye patch I wore for several years to correct my wandering vision.

* * *

My only friends as I grew up were Nathaniel and Moses, the Mennonite boy who delivered our eggs. Every Wednesday morning I would go down to the kitchen, put on the boys' clothes he had given me, and wait outside the kitchen door to go on his rounds with him. I attracted much less attention in his clothes than I did the first few times I went out with him in my regular dresses.

Moses was a great talker. He liked nothing better than to hand me the reins, lean back with his elbows on the wagon rim, and talk. He lived with his mother and six sisters in a one-room house in a Mennonite community outside of the city. His father had fallen off a roof the year before and died, so he was the man of the house now, Moses told me solemnly, his big head nodding up and down, his lower lip thrust out. He went to church in the mornings and school in the afternoons, but the eggs, which he used to do with his father, were now his responsibility and he liked it just fine. Every morning before the sun came up, he collected them, candled them, washed them in vinegar and water, packed them into baskets filled with straw, and every Wednesday drove the ten miles to Winnipeg to deliver them. It took him two and a half hours to get to Winnipeg, almost three hours to deliver his eggs around the city, and another two hours to get back, but he never complained.

I know now that Moses was an old man in a young man's body— solid, reliable, unimaginative, but I loved hearing about his world because it helped me hold on to mine. I didn't tell him much about our life on Armstrong's Point. I didn't have to. He could see that we lived in a twenty-one-room mansion with liveried servants and horses whose sole purpose was our pleasure.

I told him instead about my real home, a one-room affair, just like his, in Russia. I told him that my father, too, had fallen off a roof, that we had a cat and goats and chickens and a vegetable garden. In my real home.

* * *

I never stopped wondering about Mamma and Pappa but as the years went by, I did stop asking about them. I stopped running to the door when the Count came home with the mail. I stopped asking Esther where they were, when they were coming. She always said she didn't know and changed the subject.

At eight years old, I started spending time with the servants. While Esther was upstairs learning the fine arts of dissembling and needle-point, I was downstairs learning to gut chickens, to take scuff marks off shoes, to use a sewing machine and to iron, which I still love to this day. I would sit on the floor in front of Agnes's ironing board, inhaling the crisp smell of starch and steam, marveling as she created order and beauty from tangled messes. At first she let me do only the easy things—sheets and napkins. By the time I was ten, I was ironing the Count's shirts, the Countess's silk pleated blouses. I have Agnes's ironing lessons to thank for my first job in Manhattan.

Agnes was a homely little person, tiny, with no neck, her thin brown hair pulled into a bun so severe you could see her scalp through it. Because she was so short, she'd had one of the yardmen trim the legs of her ironing board. I found bending over her board harder and harder as the years went by.

"You have beautiful hands," Agnes told me once as she watched me gliding the iron across a skirt of the Countess's. "Just like the rest of you."

I glanced at her to see if she meant it. No one had ever called me beautiful.

"You're like a puppy still," she laughed. "You just haven't grown into your beauty."

* * *

I went back to Winnipeg when Agnes died. I didn't tell Esther I was there and spent most of the day worrying that I would run into her, much as I'm spending my days now worrying that I'll run into Nathaniel. I sat in the vaulted, echoing nave of the church with Agnes's extended family and friends and many of the servants I had known in Winnipeg. They seemed as pleased to see me as I was to see them.

Over the years, they had become so comfortable with me that they had stopped censoring themselves. I remember how they laughed and teased and touched each other; how they ate everything on their plates with gusto instead of leaving half the meal because, according to the Countess, it was the polite thing to do. I remember how they haggled over who would get to take what home when our platters of food came down to the kitchen almost as full as they had been when they went up.

"It's my day for the meat," Hattie said one day to Cook as she transferred leftover roast beef from our luncheon to a bowl her sister would pick up later.

"You had the meat yesterday," Cook said.

"But there was almost no meat left," Hattie complained. "I have five little ones to grow. It's not fair."

* * *

A few weeks after that incident, the Count asked me to join him in his library. He sat quietly while I fidgeted. I thought no one had noticed that I had been hiding my meat under my vegetables, and I was afraid to tell him the truth when he asked me why I was doing it. I thought it might get Hattie into trouble; that they might want me to stop going down to the kitchen. I finally took a deep breath and blurted it out.

"It's not fair," I ended. "We have so much and they have so little. I was just trying to help. Please don't be angry."

He looked at me with such tenderness that I thought for a moment he was coming over to hug me. But he didn't. He walked to a bookcase, ran his hand along a series of leather-bound volumes, and pulled out a thick burgundy one.

"I'm not angry, Anna. In fact, I'm proud of you," he said, coming over to me with the book. "You have a social conscience."

"What's a social conscience?" I asked.

"It means you care about people who are less fortunate than you are. The saints were that way. Some politicians are as well. It's a good thing," he said, placing the book, *The Book of Saints and Goodly Works,* in my hands. "This may be a little advanced for you, but I think it's time you started reading the books in my library and getting a real education. Come in whenever you want and read whatever you want."

* * *

The first time I went into the Count's library on my own was overwhelming. There were so many books on the shelves I couldn't see the wallpaper behind them: atlases, books on religion and history, medical texts, volumes on art and archeology, many so heavy I could barely lift them. But it was the international magazines and newspapers that captured me—*Harper's New Monthly, Century Magazine,* the American dailies. I would lie on my stomach on the red oriental carpet reading about Grace Greenwood and Nellie Bly; articles on workers' rights and sexual freedom and the vote for women. It made me feel the way I did when I sat at the tracks with Nathaniel watching the trains go by: a tightening in my stomach, a quickening of my heart, a sureness that there was something, far away from Winnipeg that I longed for. I imagined myself standing at the top of a set of stairs in front of a grand building with lions on the balustrades, speaking passionately about safe working conditions and birth control and the vote for women while the crowds below me clapped and cheered.

The Count sat with me sometimes, the smoke from his pipe tobacco curling up his thoughtful face. He told me that he agreed with many of what he called the modernists. He believed that workers should have rights and provided free lunches and medical care for the employees in his lumberyard. He believed that women should have the vote. They have a different view of life than men, he told me, because of their ability to procreate, but that view is as valid as any man's. The Countess didn't agree, he told me confidentially.

"You need to be kinder to her, Anna," he said, "to try and understand. She was brought up traditionally in a strict home. She is only trying to do what's best for you and Esther. She wants very much to please you."

As much as I resented her, there was always a part of me that wanted to please her too. I forced myself to speak more quietly and slowly. I tried to sit erectly at the table with my elbows by my sides. I tried not to fidget. I didn't complain when my lady's maid pulled at my tangles every morning until my scalp ached. I made her cards for her birthday and for Christmas. It never worked. No matter what I did, she never looked at me the way she looked at Esther or the Count.

When I was nine or ten, I came up with what I thought was a good plan. Every time I had the urge to jump up or interrupt, I would tighten my calf muscles, first one and then the other. I thought it would make me stop and think. I got a terrible cramp at the dinner table one day, jumped off my chair, knocked it over, hopped around hitting my leg and yelling. I caused more trouble than I would have if I hadn't tried.

• CHAPTER SIX •

I'm nervous, when I leave the hotel to go to the lawyer's office, that I'll run into Nathaniel, but it doesn't take me long to realize that he would never recognize me. The hood of my new parka surrounds most of my face, and like everyone else, I'm walking face down to stop the wet cold from getting inside my nose and freezing there.

The city has changed. The downtown is a hodgepodge now of Romanesque, Victorian, and neoclassical buildings with sophisticated-looking people coming and going, most of them better dressed than I am.

The lawyer has assured me on the phone that everything is in order; Charles had taken care of all eventualities before he died, including Esther's death. I just needed to sign the papers, he said, and the large part of Esther's estate is mine, leaving me wondering who got the least part.

Despite my sheepskin mitts, my hands are cold on the way back to the hotel. I stop inside City Hall to warm them up. It's like being transported back in time. Everything looks the same as it did the last time I was here: an ornate circular staircase going up to the second floor, double glass doors along the halls where the Winnipeg Board of Trade and the Historical Scientific Society still have their offices. I walk along the shiny terrazzo floor, my footsteps ringing ominously, just as they did when I was ten years old, trailing behind Esther and the Count and Countess, hating what was going to happen.

"Congratulations, young ladies," the judge said after he had signed and stamped our adoption papers. "An exciting day this. The first day of your new lives as Esther and Anna Chernovski."

*   *   *

I changed my name back to Anna Grieve the day I turned eighteen. I stood in line at a city office on Thirty-Fourth Street for two hours, signed my name on four different sets of papers, and went directly to a framing shop where I had the certificate mounted in a simple silver frame with a black velvet stand on the back. It sits on the coffee table in my office now along with *Pappa's Pockets*.

*   *   *

When I get back to the hotel, Inspector McHugh is in the lobby. He's leaning back in one of the leather lounge chairs, hat off, legs apart, coat unbuttoned, his gaze faraway. He starts when I say hello. "You look warm," he says, smiling, as he stands up to hand me a large brown envelope that's been in his lap. "I thought you might want to see this. One of my men found it at your sister's house."

I look in the envelope. It's a journal. "Thank you." How thoughtful this man is being. "Do you know where he found it?"

"Somewhere in a garden shed."

"Have they found any others?"

"No."

Before I can ask any more questions, the woman at the desk sings out, "I have a phone call from Manhattan for you, Miss Grieve."

"Thank you," I call back to her. "Tell them I'm on my way." I have a flash of guilt thinking about the journal—still upstairs—that I sneaked out of Esther's house in my underwear. He'll never know about that one.

"Have you thought anymore about the dog?" the inspector asks as I turn to take my leave.

I tell him I'm still thinking about it, then take the stairs, two at a time, up to the room. It's faster than waiting for the porter to run the elevator. The phone is ringing as I enter.

"Anna? It's me. How are you?"

"Vera. I'm so happy to hear your voice. I'm managing. How are you?"

"Fine. Good. Ben's coming up for the weekend. We're going to see *Solitaire;* Alfred Hitchcock's daughter is supposed to be wonderful in it."

"Let me know," I say. "Maybe it will still be on when I get back."

"I will. Anything new about Esther?"

"I just got back from the lawyer's office. Everything's in order with her will. Charles took care of pensions for her staff, an annuity for the Sanctuary where she volunteered, and of course a large donation to her animal shelter."

"She loved her dogs," Vera says.

"She did, every last Licorice of them. He's still in the kennel, by the way. I'm not sure what to do about him."

"Maybe bring him home?"

"I don't want to, but I'm not sure of what else to do. I can't just leave him."

"I understand," she says. "Have the police found out anything more?"

"They haven't found anything to suggest it wasn't suicide."

"Do you doubt it?"

"I don't know. I'd like to doubt it. If she killed herself, I'll spend the rest of my life wondering if there was something I could have done to prevent it."

"Anna, it's possible that she did kill herself. You know that. You also know there's nothing you could have done."

"I guess I know that. Maybe I'll never know that. Let's talk about something else. Did I tell you that the officer on the case, Inspector McHugh, took me to a factory yesterday for warm clothes?" I ask. "I look like I should be hanging hydro wire or working on a garbage truck. He's being awfully nice to me. Took me for lunch."

"Do you think he's interested in you?" I can hear the tease in her voice.

"Vera! I think he feels like we're kindred spirits—his wife killed herself."

"Oh. That's too bad. I'm sorry I made a joke out of it. I guess he knows how you feel. You could use a little understanding and some looking after."

"Maybe. Makes me a little nervous though. Remember how it worked out the last time I let someone look after me?"

"He's not Oscar and you're not in Russia. Don't beat yourself up."

We say good-bye. I take my parka off and settle on the bed with the journal Inspector McHugh gave me. About a third of the way through, I find this.

Journal number twenty-two.

19 November 1900.

I called Charles's office a few moments ago to ask if Cook should keep his dinner warm. I hung up when Mrs. Bradley answered. I'm finding it very difficult to sit alone at the dinner table wondering why Charles is at the office so much and why Mrs. Bradley always seems to be there as well. Prentiss brings in dish after dish that I can barely bring myself to taste. Yesterday I told him I wasn't hungry and left the table without eating anything, Prentiss watching me like a disapproving parent. I know he tells Charles when I don't eat. Charles has commented that I've lost weight. Last week he said that maybe that's why we can't have children, perhaps it's because I'm too thin. It feels like I'm at the bottom of that greased bowl again, clawing my way to the top and slipping down before I can grasp the edge and pull myself out.

I close the journal and my eyes. I didn't know that Charles and Esther were having problems, although I had a sense that things were not right with them when she wrote and asked me to visit her in August of 1914. We hadn't seen each other then for nineteen years. I thought of her often during those years, and we did exchange letters now and then, but whenever I had a sense that Esther was in trouble, and that I should be doing something about it, I put it aside. This time, when she wrote that it had been too long, I agreed, and made my travel arrangements.

* * *

I was surprised to see so many young men in uniform as the taxi took me through the city to Esther's house. In Manhattan, other than what you read in the papers, there were no signs that a war was even going on. Most Americans didn't think it was their job to fight someone else's battle at that point and didn't join in until the war was almost over.

Charles wasn't around much while I was there. Esther said he was doing legal work for the Royal Winnipeg Rifles, she wasn't sure exactly what. But we kept ourselves busy. We picnicked at the Assiniboine and reminisced about the good times we'd had growing up: skating on the river, tobogganing down the hills. I was reminded of how charming she could be when she was well, how happy.

I sat in on one of her volunteer sessions at the Ellis Street Sanctuary for unwed mothers one afternoon. She was in a senior position by then, head of volunteer recruitment.

I chose a seat at the back of a meeting room the day of my visit. It was filled with about twenty women, most of them rich society matrons like Esther.

She stood at the front of the room, composed and elegant. "Welcome, ladies. Thank you for coming and for your interest," she said. "Before I tell you what volunteers do here, let me tell you about our clients. These are not bad girls. They're new to Canada, most of them. They've left their families at home and send most of what they make back to them. They're unskilled and lonely. It's not surprising that they would find solace in the arms of a man. We mustn't judge them badly."

Piping up from the back of the room, a woman with a fox stole around her shoulders raised her hand and said, "I know for certain that some of the girls are from good homes right here in the city."

"You may be right," Esther replied pleasantly. "Would you see me in my office after the session ends, Mrs. Gruin?"

When the session was over, Esther took Mrs. Gruin into her office. I waited in the hall until Mrs. Gruin walked out haughtily, and then I went in to Esther's office.

"What did you tell her?" I asked breathlessly. I couldn't imagine her speaking disapprovingly to anyone. She was sitting behind a large oak desk, the surface glowing, a few files here and there.

She beamed at me. "I told her that I didn't think this was the right place for her; that there are many other volunteer organizations that would be proud to have her with them."

I told her how impressed I was and could see how happy that made her. The next day, a Saturday, Esther decided that we should take lunch to Charles, who was working at his office downtown. She had Cook prepare a basket and Dennis, her chauffeur, dropped us off across from Charles's office on Donald Street. It was very hot, hotter than Manhattan had been when I left and I was sweltering in my hat and gloves. Although many women in Manhattan, including myself, had stopped dressing so formally, Esther insisted that I put them on for a trip downtown.

We were crossing Donald Street, the food in a basket on my arm, Licorice in a basket on Esther's, when a policeman approached us and asked that we, and the few other people trying to cross, wait on the sidewalk. There was a procession making its way down the middle of the street. It was a funeral procession, the policeman told us, and we had to show respect.

Gypsies, for as far as I could see, gypsies walking slowly toward us in heavy black clothes and head scarves, six men at the front carrying a long coffin covered with braided flowers.

It resonated deeply with me. I had seen gypsies in Central Park when I first arrived in Manhattan and they had always been part of our life in Podensk. They would arrive there unannounced three or four times a year, always together, always making music with their accordions and tambourines. They would settle in the fields for the few days they were with us, trade horses, tell fortunes, and then without any warning, just as they'd arrived, go on their way.

I have a picture in my mind of them leaving one cold winter morning. They put their pots and pans and parcels on their wagon and then climbed in. There must have been twenty-five of them, all wearing everything they owned—they always seemed to be wearing everything they owned, no matter the weather. As the wagon rambled off, a young mother lifted her infant son, took his diaper off, and held him over the wagon to relieve himself. We watched the little arc of urine leave his tiny body and laughed.

Esther's hand was on my arm as the procession went by. I was just about to ask her if she remembered the gypsies in Podensk when a group of uniformed soldiers pushed between us from behind and ran into the middle of the procession. They threw tomatoes at the gypsies and shouted, "Gypsies—go home! Aliens!"

As the police tried to contain the angry soldiers, Esther's grip tightened on my arm. When I turned to her, I could see that she had that look in her eyes. She didn't know where she was. I dropped my basket of food and grabbed Licorice from her. I put my arm around her and pushed my way back to the street, hoping the chauffeur was close by. He was. He drove us home, Esther pale and unfocused the whole trip. I had never seen one her episodes last that long.

"Madam is best left alone at these times," her maid explained to me as she took Esther to her room. When I went into see her the next morning, she was sitting up with a tray of tea and toast in front of her, a mauve silk bed jacket tied around her shoulders.

"Nothing to worry about, Bencke," she said brightly, "just a little migraine. I'll be up and about in no time." She didn't remember setting out to take Charles his lunch, the riot on the street.

I asked Charles later that morning if he knew about the incident. I assumed the chauffeur had told him. "She has to be careful" was all he said, and turned back to the papers on his desk. What had happened, I wondered, to the man I was so sure would take care of Esther for the rest of her life?

I still don't know why Esther wanted me in Winnipeg: whether she wanted me to see how well she was doing with the Ellis Street Sanctuary, whether she needed a witness to the fact that things were not going well with Charles. Perhaps both.

• CHAPTER SEVEN •

Charles first saw Esther at the Princess Street Opera House when she was fifteen. It would be another seven months before they actually met. The Hess Acme Opera Company was in town performing *La Traviata* for one night only and everybody who could was going. They had asked me to go with them, of course. The Countess said I wouldn't have to wear an evening gown; that she would have a simple evening suit made for the occasion. The Count said I could use his opera glasses. Esther told me I would love the story and the music. She knew I would. But I said I would be happier staying home and reading. Which was true. I didn't like opera.

Charles was in the foyer when Esther walked in, he told us later, and was smitten on the spot. It didn't surprise me then. It still doesn't. I remember how beautiful Esther looked that evening, climbing into the carriage, snowflakes melting into her blond curls, her emerald and ruby drop earrings brushing her neck every time she moved her head.

Charles found out who she was that night but didn't meet her. Those were the days when there were rules of etiquette for everything: where a gentleman could be introduced to a lady; who was allowed to make the introductions; how long you could hold eye contact.

For the next seven months, Charles went to the Strachan Street Library after work to find out what he could about my beautiful sister, Esther Chernovski. The current newspapers were easy enough, he told us. They hung spine-up over dowels in the main library room. He would lift one out, take it to one of the long tables in the center of the room, page through it, and put it back.

Back issues were more difficult. They were in the stacks, which were on the second floor, up a staircase behind the front desk. They could only be taken out one issue at a time. Charles had to go to the desk, sign a log, walk to the stacks with the librarian, find the newspaper he wanted from hundreds filed in long, sliding drawers, take it back down to one of the central tables, and when he was through, take it back to the librarian and go through the whole process again.

Early in May he read that Esther's coming-out was on June 12. He asked Mr. Winchester, the head of the legal firm where he was studying, how he could get invited. Mr. Winchester said he couldn't. A month later, Charles read that there was to be an event called the Evening of the Arts at the Sacred Hearts Church on Hargrave Street with Miss Esther Chernovski as one of the featured soloists. He stood up and danced a little circle right there on the main floor of the reading room. No one could stop him from going to a public concert.

"Didn't people look at you?" I asked him.

"I don't know," he said. "I didn't care. I was finally going to meet the woman who was to become my wife."

We were all at that concert. The Count and Countess and I arrived early to get a seat in the front, but at the last minute, the Countess said that sitting so close to Esther might make her nervous so we moved to a middle row, right behind a tall man with fine blond hair that he kept brushing out of his eyes.

Except for Esther's performance, the concert was terrible. The Count and I had a good-natured spat on the way home about whether Divinity Cromwell had been mumbling Keats or Wordsworth. But Esther, beautiful accomplished Esther, white pearl studs in her ears and a matching choker at her neck, played Opus Ten of Chopin's Etudes magnificently. When her hands finally stopped moving over the keys, everyone stood and clapped.

Esther stayed at the piano, her head down, her fingers brushing the program in her lap. I knew she was looking at her new name, Esther Chernovski. How she loved it. She'd been writing it in her journals even before the Count and Countess adopted us.

When the applause stopped, the blond man in front of us joined the line of people waiting to congratulate Esther. He was very tall and handsome in a dress uniform with gold epaulets at his shoulders. When it was his turn to congratulate Esther, he bowed, and my insides turned to jelly.

Six weeks later he came for tea. We sat in the small windowed parlor at the back looking out at the shrubs and trees; the stands of yellow daisies, red geraniums, and purple Buddleia lining the path to the river.

Tea was poured, polite questions asked and answered. Charles's parents lived in Wales where his father owned a coalmine. Charles was in Winnipeg studying law because our internship system was considered one of the finest in North America. He had an older brother, Frank, who was practicing law in Manhattan. Yes, he intended to set up his practice in Winnipeg.

I was sitting on a chair between Charles and the Countess, trying not to clink my cup in the saucer, my heart beating fast in the charged atmosphere. The Countess was smiling at Charles and the Count and Esther. She even smiled at me once or twice. Esther wasn't making eye contact with anyone, but she was glowing.

The Count asked Charles if he had enjoyed *La Traviata*.

"Not really," Charles said. "I've never been to an opera before and wouldn't have been there if Mrs. Winchester, my employer's wife, hadn't fallen ill. From what I heard that night, I'm afraid I'm not a fan."

That moment is frozen in my mind: the light from the window hitting the gold ring on the little finger of Charles's left hand; the attentive look on the Count's face; the approving look on the Countess's face. I had thought I was the only person in the world who didn't like opera, that it was a serious character flaw. To hear Charles say he didn't like opera in such a candid manner, to watch everyone responding as if he had said he didn't like lemon in his tea, was a defining moment in my life. Maybe there was nothing wrong with not liking opera. Maybe it was okay to say so. Maybe there was nothing wrong with me.

By the time Esther and Charles were formally walking out, I was convinced he could and would move heaven and earth to keep her happy.

* * *

Not that that ever stopped me from worrying about her.

One night about two months after Vera moved into my downstairs apartment in Manhattan, she was up for tea. It was raining, the pitter-patter soft and steady on the roof. I had just received a letter from Esther. I was sliding it back and forth on the table. It was all good news: she had a new dog, Charles's business was flourishing, she was doing more volunteer work, that kind of thing. But still, every time I heard from her I found myself reading between the lines to see what was wrong. I was fingering the letter when Vera came up.

"From Esther?" she asked, sitting down beside me.

"Yes."

"Is problems?" Her Russian syntax was still taking over.

"No. She says everything is fine."

"So why you sad?"

"I don't know. Every now and then it feels to me like her old fears are creeping in."

"What she fear?"

I couldn't answer her. I never really understood what Esther was afraid of. I'm not even sure she knew.

"Anna," Vera said, "she never tell you?"

"No. She would go into a kind of trance. Her eyes would focus on something in the distance. She would excuse herself from wherever we were and go up to her room. She could do it quite politely, say she was getting a headache or something equally benign. I would follow her up and sit outside her door."

"I see was hard on you."

"Yes. It was—it still is at times, like having a fist around my heart. I would ask her if she would be all right and she would say. . .she would say. . ." The words wouldn't come out of my mouth.

"You don't have to say, Anna," Vera said.

The raindrops were now hitting the open window and coming in. Cars were honking on the street below us, their tires swishing along the wet road.

"I do have to say. I've never told this to anyone and it's burning a hole in me. I would ask her if she would be all right and she would say, 'Sometimes I'm afraid I'll die of this.' I thought when Charles came into her life, he would make everything fine."

• CHAPTER EIGHT •

It's two in the morning and I'm at the hotel window again. Even though the last performance ended hours ago, the yellow marquee lights at the St. Regis Theatre are flashing, briefly illuminating each flake of dry weightless snow as it passes by.

I can't sleep. When I'm not thinking about Esther, I'm thinking about Nathaniel. I pull the desk chair to the window and wrap myself in the bedspread. There's a train going by in the distance, its whistle long and low and lonely.

We had a game we played at the tracks, Nathaniel and I. We would take turns after each train ratcheted by, making up stories about where it was going. The passenger trains and the open boxcars filled with farm machinery were easy.

"That one's going to Halifax," one of us would say, or "That one's going to Montreal." We didn't know, but it was fun making it up. It was the freight trains, with their closed boxcars, that were more difficult for Nathaniel. He would screw up his face in concentration and, as often as not, ask me to make up the story. I would go through the Count's books in my mind and come up with stories that Nathaniel loved. "That one is going to Boston with cinnamon from Madagascar,"

I would say, or "That one has silkworms from China. They're going to a fabric factory in New York."

I had just turned fourteen when we started playing that game. Nathaniel was sixteen and we were conscious of each other in a new way by then. We had stopped roughhousing and leg wrestling some time ago. If we touched accidently, we would move apart quickly and apologize. His body was still skinny and slope-shouldered, but I couldn't stop looking at his hands, the hollow at his collar bones, amazed at the new sensations in my body, certain that the same things were going on in his.

* * *

When the sun starts to bleed across the sky, I put on my parka and head out—north this time to see if the shed that Nathaniel and I found near his house in New Jerusalem is still there. There's a light dusting of snow on the ground and each footstep leaves a perfect imprint of my boots.

No large estates or ten-bedroom mansions in this part of the city, just rundown frame bungalows with cheap lawn ornaments that I find touching somehow.

New Jerusalem was such a kaleidoscope of shacks when Nathaniel lived here—no streets or avenues, just one-room shacks wedged in wherever there was space. They were made of scrap metal, wood, tar-paper, cardboard, whatever people could get their hands on. Chickens and goats wandered around as confident that they belonged as everyone else. It's changed now, cheap prefabricated bungalows lined up precisely along icy dirt lanes.

I can't believe the shed will still be there, but I keep walking. If I'm remembering correctly, it was about a half hour from Nathaniel's house.

And then I see it, a forlorn-looking bump in a field of snow surrounded by colorless tall grasses, looking exactly the way it did when we first saw it. My eyes fill with tears as I push through the brittle weeds.

A feral cat runs out the gap where the door used to be. Inside it smells of cat urine.

Nathaniel and I stumbled on the shed when I was ten and he was twelve. We'd been having another of our contests, walking along the railway track, arms out for balance, to see who could stay on longest. We weren't paying much attention to where we were, and when we looked up, realized we were further away from his house than we'd ever been. Except for a little shed in the distance, the field was desolate. We stomped our way through the hip-high snow to get to it, just as I am doing now.

It's a square building, maybe ten feet by ten feet, made of large gray concrete blocks with a low tarpaper roof and two small openings high on one wall to let the light in. We decided, because of the odd feather here and there, that the place must have belonged to a chicken plucker.

Months later, when we were pretty sure nobody else knew about it, we claimed the shed as ours. It was a magical place; the concrete blocks kept the temperature bearable all year long and the mosquitoes never came inside. We never knew why.

The mattress we found rolled up in a corner is still there, the burlap cover I made in place although the color has bleached out; the few remaining bright spots are now a purple blue rather than the original green. There are pools of water on the floor beneath where the roof hangs in. The chair that Nathaniel took so long to re-cane is gone.

He worked so hard on it. He wet the cane and tied it to the wooden slats around the frame of the seat, then wove the strands in and out, in and out. He ripped it out three times before he was satisfied. When it was done, he asked me to try it. We laughed when I fell right through.

We spent long hours there, tickling each other and leg wrestling and playing our truth game, which involved telling each other the funniest thing that ever happened to us, the scariest thing, the saddest. The only rule was that it had to be the truth.

I told him about the day Mamma took us to the train station. That was the saddest for me.

He told me about the day his grandmother cut off the tip of his index finger. That was his scariest. She did it so the Russian soldiers wouldn't abduct him; they didn't want boys who couldn't pull a trigger.

"Did it hurt?" I asked.

"I can't remember," he said. "It happened so quickly. She took me outside and asked me to put my finger on a tree stump and it was done before I knew what had happened. It throbbed afterwards, for a long time."

* * *

Although I didn't know it until I saw Nathaniel and his family on the steamer from St. Petersburg, his family had left Podensk when we did. They had paid a government man ten dollars for one hundred and sixty acres of prime farmland in Moosomin, about two hundred miles from Winnipeg. Nathaniel brought the poster the government had given them to the shed one day. *The Last Best West,* it said on top in large black block letters. Below the lettering was a drawing of a ruddy-faced farmer in a red plaid shirt standing in front of waist-high golden wheat fields, hands on his hips, chest out. There was a dog at his feet and a big yellow sun in the background.

The government man told them they would have to clear the land to grow wheat like that. He didn't tell them it would be such back-breaking labor that one of their horses would die trying to uproot a poplar.

He told them the land was so beautiful and flat, that they would be able to see forever. He didn't tell them that they wouldn't be able to keep their eyes open. In winter they had to close their eyes to white-out blizzards. In summer to mosquitoes.

Nobody told them about the loneliness either. Nathaniel's family, like ours, was used to Podensk, where the homes radiated out from the synagogue where everyone gathered to gossip and watch the children grow. There were no houses near them in Moosomin, no synagogue, no neighbors. They found themselves watching for itinerant peddlers who arrived on no fixed schedule.

Nathaniel's family didn't stay in Moosomin long. His mother died in labor a year after they arrived, and they didn't have the will to con-tinue. Their land reverted to the Dominion because they didn't fulfill their contract.

He brought that to the shed too. He wouldn't let me touch it. It was very thin paper, with fancy lettering on top and official-looking stamps and a picture of a woman he told me was the Queen of England. His father had signed it at the bottom with a shaky X.

To be granted title to the land, it said, the settler had to live on the land for three years, cultivate thirty acres, and build a permanent dwelling. Nathaniel's family didn't meet any of the requirements.

They went back to Winnipeg, to the shtetl where most of the east-ern European Jews who couldn't tolerate the harsh prairies ended up. His father got a job as a signaler with the railway. His grandfather bought an ox and a wagon and traveled the province sharpening knives and selling dry goods like he had in Podensk. His grandmother never forgave either of them.

* * *

Standing at the window, watching the marquee blink, I remember how Nathaniel and I loved the St. Regis Theater, how we would sit across the street and watch the performers arrive and cart their paraphernalia to the back door. We saw a caged lion once and a cage full of birds.

We decided one day to sneak in and see Black Minnie and her Traveling Troubadours. We'd watched them arrive and heard their act through the windows—banjos and deep voices and tap dancing. We tried to shuffle in with the crowd after the first intermission but an usher caught us, so we went around the back and climbed through an open basement window—Nathaniel first and then me. We landed on our hands, Black Minnie's pointy black shoes right there in front of our noses. She grabbed Nathaniel by the front of his shirt and pulled him up so they were nose to nose. Nathaniel was tall by then, but she was taller. His feet didn't touch the ground when she picked him up.

"If you don't get your white ass out of here right now," she said, "I'm going to make it black and blue." His face grew very tense. I didn't know if he was angry or trying not to laugh. She put him down and he turned to climb back out through the window, but Black Minnie grabbed the back of his shirt and shoved him toward the door.

We ran back to our little shed, laughing so hard we were out of breath by the time we got there. Everything was funny it seemed: my ankles in my too-short pants, Black Minnie's tiny, pointy boots, her referring to Nathaniel's white ass.

We collapsed on the mattress and fell into each other's arms. I could see the drops of perspiration on Nathaniel's upper lip, his curly reddish chest hair peeking out of his shirt where the top button was undone. His breath was sweet and warm.

I might have had a momentary flash of knowing that this was forbidden. I might have. What I remember most is the overpowering completeness of my response. Sometimes still when I least expect it, Nathaniel's face that first time will come back to me and I can see, as clearly as I can see my own hand in front of me now, the look on his face the first time he saw my breasts.

• CHAPTER NINE •

"I hear it's raining," Vera says when I pick up the phone.

I laugh. "How do you know?"

"I'm prescient," she says.

"Let me call you back," I say. "I'm dripping all over the carpet." I hang my jacket over the shower rod, strip down to my underwear, wrap myself in my robe, and get comfortable on the bed.

"How do you know it's raining?" I say when Vera answers.

"The woman at the front desk told me. I didn't think it rained there, only snowed."

"Well, this isn't really rain. It's more like slush falling from the sky. It sticks to your eyelashes and seeps into your bones."

"How are you doing?"

"I'm managing. Just got back from the funeral home. They won't set a date until the coroner's report is in."

"So you won't be back by Friday."

"No."

"That's too bad. You'll miss the opening of Margaret's new clinic. She dropped by yesterday. She was hoping you could be there. I told her what's going on. I hope you don't mind."

"No, not at all. I won't be back in time. It feels like I'll never be back, like I never left."

"Anything new on the case?"

"Not really. I'm still having trouble believing that Esther just walked in front of a train. I've asked Inspector McHugh if I could speak to the witnesses. There were two of them apparently."

"What did he say?"

"He says he can't do it."

"I'm not sure what good it will do, Anna, but if you need to do it, ask him again. You seem to have his ear."

* * *

Inspector McHugh stops his car in front of a canary yellow bungalow on Beatrice Street and squints out the window to see if the house number matches the one on the slip of paper in his hand.

"Your car seems to be better this morning," I say, pretending I'm not aware that he hasn't said a word to me since he picked me up. He ignores my comment, turns the car off, and walks up a weather-beaten wooden ramp over the front stairs of the bungalow. When I catch up with him, he's leaning over and shaking hands with a heavy-set man in a wheelchair.

"Mr. Terrence," he says, "this is Miss Grieve, the sister of the woman you saw at the train station. Thanks again for agreeing to talk to us."

"I'm sorry for your loss, Miss Grieve," the man says, then executing a perfect turn on the spot, he wheels down a short hall to a small pale blue living room with a low white fireplace along the entire length of the back wall. The mantel is crowded with black-framed pictures of fresh-faced men in uniform.

When he sees me looking at them, he explains, "My buddies from the Great War. All gone now."

"I'm sorry, Mr. Terrence."

"No mind," he says and parks in front of two wing chairs facing out from the fireplace. "We all have our crosses to bear. Please sit down."

"I wonder if you could go over what you saw again for Miss Grieve," Inspector McHugh asks when we're seated. His voice is tight, the words clipped.

"I was at the station with George."

"George?" I ask.

"My buddy George Kaldas. We're train buffs. Go to the station every Wednesday, sometimes Thursday too. That's when the new 7-1500s come through. They're really something. Lots going on that day. All kinds of people coming into town for If Day. Your sister's train was forty-eight minutes late. Got in at five-eleven. A problem with the weather in Minneapolis, they said. She got off the train and stopped. Looked frightened. Dropped her parcels and ran across the station, right onto the track. Train coming through, I already told the police," he says, glancing briefly at Inspector McHugh. "Coal for the armament smelters in the east. Go at one hell of a speed. Don't stop here. We would have tried to stop her, but there wasn't time. I'm sorry, Miss."

"Are you satisfied?" Inspector McHugh asks when we're back in the car.

"It still doesn't make sense to me," I say. "You read her journal. You said yourself she didn't sound suicidal. Maybe the other witness will have more information."

"We're not seeing the other witness," he says curtly, putting the key in the car. "I'd have trouble explaining the rules I've broken up to now."

I'm embarrassed at having pushed him so far.

* * *

I go down to the hotel restaurant for dinner. I've been here for four days and they're already treating me like a regular. The hostess doesn't ask anymore if someone will be joining me; she just takes me to the small corner table every time, removes the extra place setting, and brings me grapefruit juice and black coffee in the morning and a glass of red wine at dinner.

Afterwards, I go upstairs and try to read. I've picked up a copy of *My Ántonia* at a local bookstore. My copy at home is falling apart I've read it so often, but even Jim Burden's poignant memories of Ántonia, which remind me of my feelings for Nathaniel, don't distract me.

I put on my parka and go out. It's a calm evening, just starting to get dark. No wind. The sky is clear and there are no storm clouds in the distance. I head to the industrial area on the outskirts of the city where Nathaniel and I used to watch the farrier and the rubber boot maker. They would give us remnants—old pieces of plywood, rubber bits—for our shed. The area is an icy, muddy field now with a few brick walkways going nowhere. Surprisingly, Hank's Carriages is still standing. The bricks are crumbling. Pigeons perched in the empty window frames scatter as I approach. Even so, the structure looks much as it must have the day Charles picked up his new carriage and came to the house to propose to Esther.

* * *

We didn't know he was coming to propose that day. He had told us only that he was coming over with a new carriage. I ran to the door when I heard hooves on the drive and watched his high-stepping horse pull the shiny red brougham up to the front door. A small brass plaque at the base of the chassis read Hank's Carriages, Winnipeg.

Charles had told me he would take me for a ride after he and Esther had their outing that day but he didn't mention it when he arrived. He told Stevens he would keep his hat and stood in the foyer, his hat in one hand, smoothing his hair back with the other.

An hour after he and Esther left, I heard the front door open and saw Esther running up the stairs. I went to the window and watched Charles retreat down the driveway.

Some time later, when Esther still hadn't come down, I went up.

"Please go away, Bencke," she said when I knocked at her bedroom door. I slid down the wall to wait. Two hours later, she opened the door. Her eyes were red. I climbed up on the bed with her. She put her head on my shoulder.

We sat for a few moments and she said quietly, sadly, "Charles asked me to marry him."

"That's good, isn't it?" I couldn't imagine what the problem was.

"I can't marry him, Bencke."

"You can't marry Charles?"

"Do you know what he did the night of my coming-out?"

"Charles wasn't at your coming-out, Esther," I said, thinking her memory was playing tricks on her again.

"He was. He was in the stand of maples across the street. He wedged himself in and stood there until his foot fell asleep. He told me he went home thinking he wasn't good enough for me."

"That's no reason not to marry him, Esther. He's told us how much he wanted to meet you. He would have come to your party if he could have."

"He felt guilty all this time for not telling me that he had spied on me that day," she said.

"Well, that's good too, isn't it? He's being honest."

"I can't marry Charles, Bencke. I can't marry anybody." She sounded so hopeless.

"Why?"

She waited a few moments. "I'm afraid to have children."

"Why?" I asked, wondering what on earth was going on in her mind.

"Because somebody might hurt them."

"Why would anybody hurt them?"

"Because my children would be Jewish. People hurt Jews."

"That doesn't happen anymore, Esther," I said. "The Count told us all that is changing. Mr. Zimmerman is on the bench now for the police court and the Count's club has just accepted three Jews."

"You're so naïve, Bencke," she replied. "Maybe you're better off that way."

"Wait," I said and ran out of the room to get the latest *Harper's Magazine* from the Count's library.

"Look, Esther," I said, showing her an advertisement with an illustration of a small rubber cap in a woman's hand. "It's called a womb veil. I don't know exactly how it works, but it prevents pregnancies. They call it a 'wife's little secret' because the husband never knows it's there."

Esther looked at me with surprise.

"Do you love him, Esther?" I asked as she was looking at the advertisement.

"Yes," she said.

"Then marry him. I know you'll be happy. Remember when you were afraid to skate and then got so good at it?"

"I'm not as good as you are."

"No, but you did it and you're glad you did. And look how you've progressed at the piano. You were nervous about that too at the beginning."

I could see her face relaxing a little, the creases at the corners of her eyes smoothing out.

"Remember when we were little and we would walk to the castle with Mamma?" I asked.

"Yes."

"Remember how I would try and walk in step with you?"

"I don't remember that." She smiled.

"You don't remember anything, silly goose. You used to get mad at me for copying you so I had to try and walk *out* of step with you, which was very much harder."

She laughed and leaned her head back on the headboard. "You won't betray me, Bencke. You won't tell Charles or anyone about this conversation."

I promised I wouldn't, wondering if she, like me, was thinking about the times I *had* betrayed her.

* * *

The first betrayal happened when Esther had just turned twelve. She came home from a hayride with friends with that vacant look on her face and I knew something was wrong. I followed her upstairs and waited for about twenty minutes outside her door until she let me in.

When we were settled on her bed, I asked how the hayride was; how many farms they went to, how large the pumpkins were.

She looked up at me and shook her head sadly.

"You can't remember all of it, can you?" I asked.

"No," she said and the tears started. "Something is the matter with my brain, Bencke. Sometimes I'm afraid I'll forget my own name."

"So that's why you sometimes think your name is Esther Chernovski," I said, remembering seeing that in her journals.

Her expression changed to disbelief. "You've been reading my journals," she said. She became very good at squirreling her journals away after that.

* * *

The next betrayal was more serious. It happened in mid-April, almost three years after the first one. Esther asked me to go for a walk with her along the Assiniboine at the back of our property. She hadn't suggested anything like that since she discovered I was reading her journals, and I was on my best behavior.

The mosses were soft underfoot and the wild irises were just starting to peek up through the winter debris. We walked to an old uprooted tree trunk that we used to sit on. It was close to thirty feet long, white with age. I brushed off a few dead leaves and we sat down. Esther pulled her shawl close and sat worrying at the buttons on her glove.

"I need to ask you something," she said after a few moments.

"Yes?"

"You have to promise me that you won't tell anybody."

"I'm sorry I read your journals, Esther," I said and promised her, meaning it at the time, that I wouldn't tell anybody what she was about to tell me this time.

We sat for a few moments listening to the water flowing in the river, the squirrels rummaging under the leaves.

"Do you ever get the feeling that it's not really you talking?" she asked.

"What do you mean?"

"Well, sometimes it feels like the words coming out of my mouth are not mine. Do you feel that way?"

I could tell she wanted me to feel that way, but I didn't want to lie to her. "No," I said, "I don't feel that way, but I'm not surprised you do, given the way the Countess expects us to talk to people."

She shook her head. "That's not it. It's like I'm not there. As if I'm outside or above, watching everything and then the room gets small and shoots away from me. I'm afraid I'm losing my mind, Bencke."

I chewed on our conversation for days. I was old enough to know that Esther needed help that I couldn't give her, but I had given her my word. My concern for Esther won.

I finally approached the Countess. She was at her writing desk, her back to the door. I waited until she turned to me.

"Yes, Anna," she said, putting down her pen. "Come in."

My throat closed. I hated her straight back and her perfect hair. I hated her for not knowing there was something wrong with Esther, for not taking care of her, for not loving me.

I turned and walked away.

Two days later I went to see the Count. He was at his desk in the library, engrossed in a book on his lap, his teeth around his pipe.

"Come in, Anna," he said, putting his pipe in an ashtray. He listened with his head down, hands steepled over his nose, as I told him what Esther had told me. When I was through, he looked up.

"It must have been difficult for you to tell me this," he said. "I suspect it feels like you're betraying Esther, but in time you'll see that just the opposite is true. You're displaying great love for your sister's well-being. You're right to ask for help."

Dr. Ridout came the next day. When he left, the Count explained to me that he had said Esther's experience was common in young women of her age; their bodies are ready to have children although they're not emotionally or mentally prepared. He said it would pass when she was married and prescribed drops for the interim.

The Count told me I should stop worrying, that he was sure the drops would work and that it was not my job to take care of Esther, that I couldn't even if I wanted to.

I'm sure I stopped blinking when he said that. It had never occurred to me that it wasn't my job to take care of Esther.

By the time preparations began for Esther's coming-out a year later, a distance had grown between us. Esther, betrayed, had stopped confiding in me. And I, given permission to stop taking care of her, resolved to try. I stopped looking for her journals and rarely sat outside her room. I even convinced myself that I didn't have to worry about her. From what I could see, the drops Dr. Ridout had prescribed were working. She seemed happily caught up with the rest of the house in the preparations for her coming-out.

Imported orchids cocooned in newspapers arrived at the conservatory in white, windowless trucks. Chamber music groups, at least two a week, auditioned in the large drawing room. Maids scrubbed the wallpaper down with dough, washed the draperies, and spread them on the grass at the back of the estate to dry in the sun. Dressmakers with straight pins in their teeth measured and pinched and pulled and stood back and clucked. Esther and the Countess, and sometimes even the Count, nodded and approved and smiled.

Fifty-four years later, sitting on a bed in the Fort Garry Hotel in Winnipeg with a box of winter clothes on the luggage rack at my feet, I find out that Esther had not been enjoying any of it.

Journal Number Nine
4 December 1888.
I lost myself again at the fitting just now and excused myself to go

upstairs. I could feel a headache coming on as well. Everyone else seems to be so energized by all these preparations. How I hate them. I knelt at the side of the bed when I got to my room and prayed to God to make the headache stop but the pink roses on my wallpaper had already grown in size and become blood red and were dancing towards me humming, humming, like a swarm of bees. I want to run when this happens. I want to die. Anything to stop my heart from beating this way and my head from throbbing. I got into bed and pulled the covers over my head. An hour later, I must have fallen asleep, l opened my eyes. The roses were back on the wall, pink and pretty and placid.

Similar entries follow, some as painful to read, a few positive entries about her piano lessons and outings with friends. A lot about anti-Semitism: the government is considering putting a quota on the number of Jews allowed in Manitoba; thugs broke into a dry goods store owned by a Jewish couple and forced them to get down on their knees and kiss the Union Jack. *The Wall Street Journal* says that sixty-five percent of Americans think that Jews are greedy, dishonest, and pushy.

I'm surprised to read that Esther went back to the fortune-teller on her own shortly after our visit. She didn't tell me about it. The fortune-teller told her there would be tragedy in her life and that the angels could save her.

I sit with her journal in my lap wondering what else I hadn't known over the years, whether I would have done anything differently if I had known, and whether it would have made any difference.

* * *

Three years after Esther's coming-out, when her life and mine had settled into predictable, separate routines, everything changed. I knew I needed the Count's help again.

"Anna," he said when he saw me at the door to his library. He lifted a slim magazine from his lap to show me. "I was just thinking about how much you would enjoy this. We've been talking about slavery and human rights for some time now. This is a compendium of articles on slavery that goes back to the sixteen hundreds. Fascinating."

"Do you mind if I close the door?" I asked, my heart pounding in my ears.

"Not at all," he said. My legs felt like weights as I walked across the room, aware that he was watching my every step. When I was seated across from him, he waited, a concerned look on his face. I cleared my throat and rubbed the back of my neck. I took deep breaths and finally began.

I watched his face go from incredulity to confusion to disappointment.

"Who is the father?" was all he said.

"I don't want to tell you, please."

* * *

When everything was arranged and my passage booked, I went to the shed to see Nathaniel. Unless one of us couldn't get away, we met there most afternoons. For almost a week, since the day I approached the Count, I hadn't shown up.

Nathaniel was sitting on the mattress, leaning against the wall, a blanket over his lap. "Where have you been?" he asked, lifting the blanket so I could climb under with him. "Come. It's getting chilly. I was worried about you." He was so pleased to see me.

I stood at the foot of the mattress looking down. I was afraid I would cry if I looked at him.

"What's the matter, Anna?"

"Nothing." I shook my head and then cocked it. "I think there's a train coming."

Nathaniel listened. "I don't hear anything."

"I don't *hear* it," I said. "I *feel* it."

He went to the door. "It reminds me so much of Moosomin here. It was so beautiful there between the two valleys."

"How can you say it was beautiful after everything that happened there?"

He turned back to me, confused. "You know why I loved it there, Anna. We owned land, for as far as we could see, farther even. Can you imagine?"

"You think owning land is everything, Nathaniel." I hated the way I was acting but couldn't seem to stop. "Maybe you should have stayed in Moosomin if you loved it so much."

He put his arms around me. I shrugged him off.

"What's wrong?"

"Nothing. I'm going away for a while, that's all."

"You're going away?"

"Yes."

"Where?"

"I can't tell you."

"When?"

"Soon."

"Soon?

"Why are you repeating everything I'm saying?"

"When are you coming back?"

"I don't know."

"You don't know?"

"No."

"I thought we were going to get married and live on a farm and have children."

"We never really said so," I replied.

"Not everything has to be said out loud."

"I think it does."

"Then say it. Tell me out loud why you're leaving me."

"Nathaniel, I'm not leaving *you*."

"You're not?" he asked. "Then how come you haven't told me before that you're going away or asked me to come with you?" A gust of cold air rushed when he opened the door to leave. "My grandmother's right," he said. "You're as crazy as your mother."

• CHAPTER TEN •

I've worked with a lot of pregnant women in my years in Manhattan—married women, single women, colored, white, and Asiatic women, women having their first child or their ninth, women with husbands and nannies, women without husbands working as nannies. They all had one thing in common: they didn't want to be pregnant.

I didn't want to be pregnant either, but I can't deny that I was thrilled that my pregnancy was taking me to Manhattan.

The Count went there shortly after we spoke and found a place for my confinement—the Stuyvesant Guesthouse in Murray Hill. It was in a respectable part of the city, he told us when he came back, women-only, many of them with my special needs. With the dates settled, he found a widow in Winnipeg to travel to Manhattan with me, stay for the duration, and escort me back. He even arranged a hospital birth.

Other than letting me know that it was all taken care of, the Count and Countess didn't ask how I was feeling, tell me what to expect, or give me advice, and they studiously avoided looking at my waistline. Esther did her best. She found a book in the Count's library called *The Diseases of Women* and read aloud to me, with great gravity, from the two sections on pregnancy. One section was on the birth chair, which she said sounded very good because it had arms to grip during contractions. The other section was on the medicalization of pregnancy. She wasn't sure how she felt about that.

I didn't have the heart to tell her that the book, which was written in 1777, was hopelessly outdated.

When I think back on my pregnancy now, I don't remember any maternal feelings. I do remember feeling embarrassed that people would know what I had done when they saw my shape changing. But I remember being fascinated with the changes in my body—my tender breasts and swelling nipples. And I was hungry, almost all the time. I controlled myself at mealtimes and went downstairs often, where Agnes would make me scrambled eggs and French toast, the foods I craved.

I didn't grieve that I would never know my baby. That didn't come until years later. I did grieve, and probably still do, that my relationship with Nathaniel was over. I could never tell him that I was pregnant and was giving our baby up for adoption. He wouldn't have accepted it. And I couldn't just pretend it never happened. Our relationship had been so pure, so direct. I knew it couldn't continue that way with an unspoken secret like this between us.

* * *

My companion, Mrs. Valentina Miller, and I didn't talk much on the trip to Manhattan. She read a great deal and knitted. I spent most of the time looking out the window at what I thought of as Nathaniel's land: endless, colorless, fields; flattened grasses in ditches; farmhouses so far back they looked like dollhouses; small towns that all seemed to have the same skinny dog barking after us as we left the station.

Three days after we boarded, the attendant knocked and told us that we were arriving at Grand Central Station. We were in the car behind the engine. I pulled the window down and stuck my head out, eager to see the soaring glass and steel structure I had read so much about. Instead, I found myself watching, in horror at first, as a brakeman in gray overalls stepped out from the back of the engine—the train was still moving—leaned over and uncoupled the engine from the rest of the cars. The engine went off on a track to the left and the rest of the cars, ours in front, glided silently and regally into the station. It was called a flying switch, I found out later, done to make the engine immediately available for another train and to make the entrance into Grand Central seamless and smokeless.

It was the first thing I fell in love with about New York.

* * *

I established a routine at the Stuyvesant immediately. I rose at six and went down to the dining room for breakfast in the outfit I had bought on the Lower East Side the day after we arrived—black wool men's pants, a black frock coat, white suspenders over a white shirt, and a large-brimmed black hat. I'd decided, even before we arrived, that I'd be more comfortable and anonymous in men's clothes, just as I was when I went around the city with Moses the egg boy and Nathaniel.

"If your husband would prefer," the shopkeeper said when I chose my outfit, "we could find a pair of black suspenders."

I told him it was all perfect, asked if I could try it on, and wore my new clothes back to the guesthouse. Nobody, other than the shopkeeper, gave me a second look. With my hair tucked under my hat, my height and long stride, I looked like all the orthodox Jewish men I had seen in Winnipeg and now saw on the streets here.

Three other people were staying at the guesthouse when I was there. One was a mousy brown-haired woman in her forties, appropriately called Miss Brown. I never heard her say a word. She had her toast and tea in the morning, washed her cup and saucer, and went out. I didn't see her again until the next morning. There was another woman about Esther's age; Mrs. William Alfred Pine from South Carolina, she said. Like me, she had a female companion whose name I never learned. It became clear as the months went by that Mrs. Pine and I were in the same condition. She tried several times to engage me in conversation, suggesting we have lunch, take in a show, do some shopping. Her slow, Southern drawl made me impatient for her to finish her sentences so I could get on with my exploring.

By the time I gave birth, I had explored Manhattan from Harlem to the financial district, from the Upper West Side to the Lower East Side. I walked main streets, side streets, cul-de-sacs, and lanes. I ate oysters from carts at the harbor and hot dogs from wagons in Greenwich Village. I watched dockworkers loading ships at the South Street seaport and bouncers throwing drunks from bars in Times Square. I rode the carousel at Coney Island, bought flowers from the market at Union Square. I even got up the courage to go into Delmonico's once, a strictly male enclave at the time. I left as soon as the maître d' approached me. I smile every time I go there today; they greet me with such respect.

In a few short months, I think I saw more of Manhattan than most people who live here do in a lifetime. Mrs. Miller, after a few half-hearted tries at getting me to stay in, or at least confine myself to the neighborhood, gave up. I think she may have been relieved to have the time to herself.

My favorite spot then, as it is now, was Central Park. I arrived there most days just before noon and ate the sandwiches the guesthouse had prepared for me as I watched what I thought of as the noon show.

This place is a marvel, I wrote to Esther. *There's one path for carriages only. They're not going anywhere, simply driving in the Park to be seen. The horses are beautiful and high-stepping. I think they get their coats brushed more often than I brush my hair. They wear blinkers and look straight ahead. The liveried drivers look straight ahead too and so do the people in the carriages. They are so stuck-up, Esther. Then there's a separate path for people on horseback and another one for people on foot, mostly office workers taking their lunch break. Then thirty-five feet away, there are gypsies cooking on open fires and hanging their laundry from lines they've strung between trees. They're just like the ones that came to Podensk, Esther. Remember them? And there's a zoo, at least that's what they call it. It has four animals—three swans and a bear that puts his nose through the bars and watches forlornly as the sheep munch their way through the park.*

I wrote to Esther fairly often in those early days and she wrote back just as often, thanking me for helping her work out her concerns about marrying Charles and telling me about their wedding plans. He was building a house for her on the banks of the Assiniboine, very near the Count and Countess's. He had bought her a Springer spaniel and she named him Licorice, which was his favorite candy. She understood that I couldn't come to the wedding because of my condition.

After my lunch at Central Park, I usually walked to the Astor Library on Lafayette, my white suspenders stretching farther apart on my belly as the months went by. It was a forty-five-minute walk if I went there directly, but most days I took a different route or stopped at Madison Square Garden to watch a bicycle race or see an operetta. I fainted once in a line waiting to see *The Merry Widow*. A young couple helped me inside and shared their oranges with me. I don't think they realized I was a woman.

What I love about New York, I wrote to Esther, *is that everybody thinks they belong. And everybody is different. I see women riding bicycles and men with earrings walking arm in arm with other men. There's one very skinny man I see often on the El with his pet monkey on his shoulder, busy picking things out of his owner's hair. Nobody even gives him a second glance. New Yorkers can be rude, but they can also be kind. Whenever I stop to look at my map, someone always stops to help me. Sometimes they walk me over to a spot where I can get a better view of where I'm going. You ask if I'm lonely. I don't have friends yet, but I go to Sachs's Cafe most after-noons after the library. It's a gathering place for intellectuals and radicals, most of them Eastern European. They're passionate about so much, Esther; equality for women, slavery, politics, and birth control. I take a book with me and pretend I'm reading, but really I'm listening to every word. I think one of the waiters here, Simon, has figured out what I'm doing. He told me the other day that Emma Goldman was at a table behind mine and asked if I would like to meet her. I said no. I don't want to meet anybody with this huge stomach of mine but as soon as it's gone, I'll become politically involved as well. I feel like I belong somewhere, Esther, finally.*

* * *

Just after dinner on the evening of June 18, my water broke. I knew what was happening, but I hadn't expected such a deluge. Mrs. Miller and I were the only ones at the dining room table when it happened. I jumped up in shock. She got me a towel and ran out for a taxi. I remember thinking as I walked down the steps of the guesthouse that the pains were not so bad, but the moment we arrived in the hospital entrance, I was hit with such a fierce contraction, I fell to my knees and threw up on the floor. Two orderlies lifted me on to a gurney and rushed me down the hall to an operating theater.

When it was over, a nurse wrapped the baby in a white blanket and whisked it out of the room. Nobody told me what sex it was or whether it had all its fingers and toes and I didn't ask. Everyone in the operating theater had treated me with such thinly veiled contempt that I didn't feel I had the right to. And at the time, I thought that the less I knew about the baby, the less I would think about it.

Since then, I've heard friends with children talk about their labors—ten hours, twelve. Mine was six so I know it could have been worse. I've heard them agree that they forgot the pain the moment they looked into their babies' eyes. I never got a chance to do that and have never forgotten the pain.

Twelve days later, swollen breasts bound with long strips of cotton, a pad of cotton between my legs, I took a cab with Mrs. Miller to Grand Central Station. We waited on the platform companionably until a porter stepped down from the train and yelled "All aboard!" He helped Mrs. Miller up the narrow steps to the vestibule and reached down for my satchel, which I was holding in front of me with both hands.

"Thank you for everything, Mrs. Miller," I yelled up at her. "I'm not going back to Winnipeg. Please tell the Count that I've found a place to live and that I have work. Thank you again, Mrs. Miller, for everything." I saw her mouth was open as I turned and left.

I can still remember the fear and anticipation I felt when I pushed open the doors to the Forty-Second Street exit. I can always go back to Winnipeg, I told myself as I walked through the veil of fetid air spewing from the breweries and factories along the street. I can always go back.

Even then I knew I wouldn't.

If Nellie Bly, twenty-three, penniless and out of work, could convince the *New York World* to hire her so she could have herself committed to a lunatic asylum for women on Blackwell's Island and expose the conditions; if Susan B. Anthony, at sixteen, could stand on street corners collecting signatures for the abolition of slavery, surely I could find a meaningful way to make my life work in the only place I've ever felt I belonged.

• CHAPTER ELEVEN •

"Anna?"

"Yes?"

"Anna Chernovski?"

I'm on the fourth floor of Eaton's in the lingerie department buying a few things to get me through the rest of the trip when a woman with a skunk-like white stripe through the middle of her black hair approaches me and smiles. I have no idea who she is.

"Take the cotton," she says. "They're more comfortable. You don't remember me, do you? It's Beatrice. Beatrice Albright. Beatrice Hooligan when you knew me."

Of course. The fake British accent, the aggressive friendliness. She was one of Esther's neighborhood friends growing up. Her family had come to Winnipeg after the War of 1812 and did everything they could, as did their descendants, to keep their children from forgetting their roots.

"Are you here visiting Esther?" she asks.

"Yes."

There's been nothing in the papers about Esther and I don't feel up to telling her.

"It's been some time since you were here, hasn't it? Twenty years or more?"

"Yes. That's about right."

"I don't know if Esther ever told you," Beatrice goes on, "but I introduced her to a few eligible widowers after Charles died. She never seemed interested in following up."

"That was kind of you. How have you been? You're looking well."

"Oh we're fine," she says, running her hand through her streak. "Fine. Harold has retired. Difficult having him around. The children are married with children of their own, of course. We have six grand-children. And you? Esther tells me you have a thriving business in Manhattan."

I do, I tell her, and get that sinking feeling in my stomach that overtakes me when I'm forced to compare my life to the lives of other women. I may be freer than many of them, I tell myself. I may even be happier, but still, I always feel like a failure for not following a more traditional path.

A perky young saleslady in a black jacket and tight skirt approaches us. "Can I help you ladies?"

"Oh no, we're fine," Beatrice says and smiles at me conspiratorially. "Remember that day the police brought you home from the Vaughan Street Jail?"

I remember it well. Beatrice and two of Esther's other friends were at the house when they brought me home that day in my boys' clothes. I'm sure they laughed about it for weeks.

It was March. A drab day, raining lightly. Nathaniel and I had been picketing in front of the Vaughan Street Jail with about ten other people. A few of them had umbrellas. The rest of us were getting wet. We were protesting the upcoming hanging of twin brothers Cosmo and

Stuart Sanna, who had been found guilty of robbing a dry goods store and beating the owner to death.

Nathaniel and I were carrying signs we had made. His said "Only God can take a life." Mine said "Hanging is murder too." I teased him about his sign. He was always more religious and proper than I was.

I was surprised when a policeman picked me out of the line of protestors and took me home. I was certain that I looked like any other North End street urchin in my boys' clothes.

It had never occurred to me that the Count and Countess were worried about my wanderings and were having me followed. The Count had tried several times to convince me that it wasn't safe to wander around on my own and suggested that our driver take me wherever I wanted to go, but I continued to sneak out and he didn't pursue the matter. I suspect now that the slight man in the long raincoat I saw so often was a detective they had hired to keep track of me. They must have relaxed when he told them that I was only on my own on the way to meet Nathaniel, that we did everything together after that.

Beatrice walks to the desk with me, a little annoyed that I'm not getting the cotton, but regains her composure. "Would you and Esther like to come for dinner while you're here?" she asks. "We'd love to have you."

I thank her and tell her we're booked for the few days I have left.

• CHAPTER TWELVE •

I did a quick check of my suit to make sure my breast milk hadn't leaked and knocked at the door of 39 Delancey Street, the house Simon had told me rented out inexpensive, shared rooms.

A squat woman in a dirty apron answered and squinted up at me. "Yes?"

"I'm interested in a room," I said, glancing at the sign in the window.

She looked me over, took a chain of keys from a pocket under her apron, and waddled down a short dark hall. "This is our largest room," she said, standing back so I could look in. "You would be sharing it with two other young ladies." All I could see were shadows. I asked if she could turn on the lights.

She sniffed. "The lights go on at eight in the evening and go off at eleven. It's not okay with you?"

"Yes," I said. "It's fine."

I tried to decipher the shapes. "There seem to be only two beds."

"Yes. One works. Two sleep. If shifts change, you double up. It's not okay with you?"

"It's okay," I said. "Is there a bathroom?"

"Yes, of course, there's a bathroom. It's on the landing between the first and second floor. If there's a key in the lock you can go in."

The room was three dollars a week. That included coffee in the morning and dinner. Toast or buns with the morning coffee was ten cents extra. I took the room with coffee only. I had fifteen dollars left, which gave me almost five weeks to find work.

Dropping my satchel in front of one of the beds, I went to the window and lifted a short curtain so I could get a better look at my new home. It was a long and narrow room, painted yellow. There was a raised pattern under the paint. I ran my fingers over it. There was wallpaper underneath—baskets filled with flowers. The two beds, cots really, were opposite each other along the long walls and had worn chenille bedspreads, mustard-colored like the curtain. Pinned up along the walls above both beds were black-and-white fashion advertisements. There was an old chest of drawers on the short wall opposite the window, shiny black, peeling. Women's underclothes were hanging out of the open top drawer.

I dropped the curtain, went to the bed where I had left my satchel, and tried to push it underneath the bed. When it wouldn't go, I got down on my knees and looked under the bed: an old wooden crate, some balled-up clothing with dust balls clinging to it, a laceless man's work boot. I took my shoes off and put them beside my satchel and lay down on the bed, hoping I wasn't disturbing any predetermined order. When I started to think about the baby and about Nathaniel and Esther, I knew I had to go for a walk.

"Dinner is at six, Miss Grieve," Mrs. Sokolov, the landlady, yelled as I passed the kitchen. "This is the first and last time I'll be telling you."

It was late Thursday afternoon, the day before Shabbos. Peddlers were pushing wagons and waving pots and pans and chickens. Children were grabbing at my skirts and playing hide-and-seek behind them. The noise was deafening. It made New Jerusalem in Winnipeg look placid.

* * *

"I think I'll skip dinner tonight," I said to Mrs. Sokolov when I got back.

"Don't expect it to come off your rent," she replied.

In my room, I unwound the wet cotton covering my breasts, listening to the dishes clattering, to bursts of laughter, to cutlery clinking. The Countess flashed into my mind for a moment, and I wondered if the people in the dining room were using the right fork.

I put my soaking cotton strips into a small bag to wash later, took fresh cotton from my satchel, wrapped it around my breasts, put on my nightgown, and hung my suit on a hanger at the back of the door. I went to the window and sat down. The house next door was so close I could have touched it if I leaned out. I sat there most of the night wondering if the beds had bedbugs, if I would find work, if the baby were a boy or a girl, if it had all its fingers and toes, if it looked like Nathaniel or me, if someone would love it.

For the next three nights, I had the room to myself. I slept, long hours, had disturbing dreams of babies in white blankets and train whistles.

My roommates, Freya and DeeDee, burst in three days later, smelling sweet and powdery like the room. They gave me the briefest of glances, climbed into the other bed together, and pulled the spread up.

Monday morning at five, I rewrapped my breasts with fresh cotton, sponged my suit, put on my hat, and walked to Hester Street, where I joined a line of women waiting for day work in the clothing factories. There must have been a hundred women in that line. It ran along Hester and around the corner along Center. Most of the women were orthodox Jews with horsehair wigs and heavy dresses and shawls. They were tired and hot in the July heat—and cranky. They closed ranks and glared at me wordlessly as I walked by.

It took two hours to reach the front of the line. "Can you sew?" a man sitting at a small table in front of the long brick building asked me. "Did you make that, for instance?" he asked, gesturing at my suit with his chin.

"Yes sir, I did," I lied, smoothing my jacket down, checking for tell-tale milk stains. "But I'd prefer ironing if there is an opening in that department."

"Department," he snickered. "You'll start on the machines like everyone else. You work on Shabbos?"

"Yes sir."

"Good girl. We'll get along just fine." He wrote a number on the corner of a page in his ledger, ripped it off, and handed it to me. "Go up to the third floor and give this to Sam. Next!"

The third floor was a long narrow room with three rows of skinny tables running end to end along its length. Sewing machines sat three feet apart in front of each table. Wooden chairs were upended on the table beside each machine. A banner along one wall of the room read "Weiner and Son, Manhattan Manufacturers of Fine Ladies' Coats."A banner under it read "No talking no laughing no unauthorized break."

Every morning at six forty-five, a whistle blew and forty-five women, myself included, shuffled up the staircase. We lifted the chairs off the tables, righted them in front of our machines, and sat down. Five minutes later three men with baskets walked between the tables and put thread, bobbins, scissors, and coat sections, cut and ready for stitching, on the tables in front of us.

At ten a whistle sounded. We pushed our chairs back and shuffled to an empty room across the hall where we rotated our heads and massaged each other's shoulders and opened and closed our fingers. Fifteen minutes later the whistle sounded again and we went back to our machines.

We had a half-hour break for lunch, when we were allowed to go outside, and a fifteen-minute afternoon break. The final whistle sounded at eight in the evening. We stood up, placed our scissors, bobbins, and thread on the tables in front of our machines, upended our chairs, and staggered out. When we were gone, supervisors went through the room with baskets and brooms. If they found anything other than useless remnants and thread around the machines or on the floor, the entire table was docked three cents a person.

If anyone talked during working hours, both parties were fined the first time and fired the second. If you happened to go into labor, which wasn't unusual in a room full of orthodox Jewish women, you were sent home and someone waiting in the line downstairs was sent up to replace you.

When Sonja, one of the workers on my shift, went into labor, I asked Sam if I could accompany her home. "You accompany Sonja home and you accompany yourself right out of a job," he told me. "Get my drift?"

Another time, when we had just come back from a break, I watched a broad-shouldered young woman walk over to an older woman and pull her out of her chair. "Take my chair again and it isn't the only thing you'll lose." I was too tired to interfere.

* * *

One Friday afternoon in August—Friday was my day off—I stopped at the corner of Eighth and West Twenty-Third to hear a soapbox speech. It was the only kind of entertainment, apart from the library, that was free.

A colored man in a stylish baggy suit and a white woman in pantaloons were standing on a small wooden stage, waving their arms and raising their voices, having a wonderful time arguing about who had it worse in America—white women or colored men. They talked about property rights, freedom of speech, employer discrimination. After about ten minutes of this, the woman turned to the man and poked him in the chest. "And when did you get the vote?" she asked.

His eyes wide with feigned surprise, he said, "On February 3, 1870. You know that."

She took her finger from his chest and lifted it in the air. "We win," she told the crowd. "Women don't have the vote yet!"

As I walked home, I was thinking about the Count—about the times we had talked about human rights and colored people.

As soon as I was in the door, Mrs. Sokolov shuffled up to me. "There's a man here to see you," she said suspiciously. "I put him in the parlor."

And there he was, looking so out of place in the shabby, over-furnished parlor with his perfectly creased pants and his shiny shoes. I was so happy to see him I welled up with tears. I think he felt much the same way, but we kept our distance and our manners. He rose when I came in and smiled and waited until I was seated before he sat down again. He told me I looked well, which was not true. My hair was frizzy, pulled back in a low ponytail, which barely contained it. I was wearing a second-hand skirt and blouse and men's shoes.

"Esther tells me you have work," he said.

"Yes, I do."

"Is it paying enough?"

"I'm managing."

I hated to see him struggling to make a connection. I could hear Mrs. Sokolov in the kitchen preparing the late dinner shift. "Would you like a coffee, Count?" I asked. I thought I would go into the kitchen and ask Mrs. Sokolov to make him a coffee and skip mine the next morning.

"No thank you, my dear. I just wanted to make sure you were all right."

I heard the front door open and then close.

"You know I've set up a bank account for you."

"Yes. Esther told me."

"You haven't touched it."

"No."

"Don't you need it?"

Two men walked by the parlor laughing loudly.

"How is the Countess?" I asked, uncomfortable with the whole situation, avoiding his question. "What is Esther's new home like?"

"They're all fine, Anna. Thank you for asking. Esther's house is wonderful. I'm sure she'd like you to see it. I'm not here to intrude on you. My fear is that you're not safe on your own. Is there anything I can do to convince you to come home?"

"There isn't," I said. "I'm sorry. I hope you can understand."

I know I must have sounded brusque. I didn't mean to. I was finding it difficult to turn him down and when I feel that way, even today, I rush to get it over with.

But it must have hurt him. He reached over to the end table beside him where he had put his hat. He stroked the fine black felt for a few moments, then picked it up, and rose from the chair. "I'm going to continue putting money into the account. Please use it if you need it. And let me know if you need anything else. Will you promise me that?"

About fifteen minutes after he left, when I knew he wouldn't be in the neighborhood, I went out for a walk. Seeing the Count had made me realize how lonely I was.

A full moon and lights in the windows were making the city glow. I could see people inside their homes eating and talking; people on the street walking in pairs, laughing, hugging each other and then parting.

The next week was difficult for me. I came closer to going back to Winnipeg than I ever had. I didn't make my sewing quota on two consecutive days and was given a warning. I lost my appetite and my desire to walk. But every time I thought about going back, I imagined Nathaniel's face when I told him about our baby. I knew I would have to tell him and that he would never forgive me. I imagined the Countess's disapproving face. And I saw Esther in my mind's eye, Esther whom I missed so very much and was still working so very hard not to worry about.

At the end of the week, I walked by Carnegie Hall on Seventh Avenue. I had watched the building going up. How wonderful, I thought, that this elegant building has been erected so people could hear beautiful music. I realized that my mood had lifted and it was time to start making plans.

* * *

Energized with a new resolve, I approached the floor foreman and asked him if I could please be switched to the ironing department. At that point, getting sore feet seemed preferable to having a sore back. He agreed and I joined eleven women in a corner where ironing boards were arranged in three circles of four each. Each group faced a round table that held sleeve and pressing boards, seam rolls, pounding blocks, tailor's hams, and rolls of brown paper, all within arm's reach of each ironing board. I was pleased that standing at the ironing board for eleven hours was not only easier on my back, it didn't bother my feet, either.

Like everyone else at Weiner and Son, I had a quota. I had to finish one hundred and twenty-six sleeves a day. That was just over five minutes per sleeve to iron the seams flat, steam the shoulders to fit into the armholes, and press a five-eighths-of-an-inch hem at the wrist so the lining could be hand-stitched in with just enough give for the elbows to bend.

I was lucky. I was paid seven dollars a week instead of the five most factories paid. My shifts were eleven hours instead of the usual fourteen. Rats were rare because a man came in every night with a bag of hungry cats. And winters were not too bad because a pot-bellied coal stove worked nonstop to keep our hands warm enough to work.

When I left Weiner and Son almost two years later, I had perfected a system that saw me doing one hundred and thirty sleeves a day, one hundred and thirty-six on a good day. They were sorry to see me go.

"You're going where?" Mrs. Sokolov asked when I told her I was leaving the rooming house.

"West Twenty-Fifth," I told her.

She sniffed. "How you're going to manage there on your salary," she said, "is none of my business."

I wasn't sure either, but I had saved enough of my meager salary to live for a month without working.

• CHAPTER THIRTEEN •

The young woman at the front desk takes the phone from her ear and waves me over. Dripping from the freezing rain, I walk self-consciously across the lobby.

Glancing down at the box of Salisbury House muffins in my hand before reaching into the message box behind her, she smiles. "Addictive, aren't they."

"They are," I say, looking down at a newspaper on the counter. "If Day Donations Climb," the headline reads. There's a picture of a bridge exploding, five or six young men in Nazi uniforms standing off in one corner of the shot.

"You weren't here for If Day, were you?" she asks, handing me the message. It's from Vera.

"No, but I heard about it. Sounds a little bizarre."

"It may have been bizarre," she says, "but it was good business. Most of the people staying here were from out of town and didn't know what was going on. They were afraid to leave the hotel. Locals who did know what was going on spent the day here to watch the action. From our front steps you could see the smoke where they faked blowing up that bridge. The anti-aircraft gunners were on top of that building right there," she says, pointing to a building across the street with a brass cupola. "Everyone had breakfast and lunch and then dinner here. People were eating in the lobby and on the mezzanine and on the steps. We actually ran out of bread."

I take the message from her and go to my room, wondering again as I watch dark wet spots forming under my boots why the hotel doesn't have rubber trays to protect the carpet. I throw my coat over the shower rod and ask the operator to call the tenants' phone in my house. It's close to six. Vera just called, so she should be there. There's no answer. I have the operator try my phone upstairs, although I don't expect Vera to be there. As close as we are, she never takes liberties with our friendship. No answer there either. I have the operator try the tenants' number again. Vera answers this time, breathless.

"Sorry," she says, "I was downstairs doing laundry and the cold water tap wouldn't turn off. What a mess!"

"Has it stopped?"

"Yes. Yes. I turned off the water main."

I lean back on the bed and take a deep breath. "Whew. For a moment I thought it was something serious. Too bad Ben isn't there yet to fix it. Is he still coming on the weekend?"

"Yes. But I don't think I should wait."

"No. Call Mr. Green. His number is in my black address book in the top right-hand drawer of my desk under W for workmen. How is everything else?

"Fine." She hesitates. "Anna, I'm calling because there's a letter here for you."

"Yes?"

"I think it's from Esther."

"From Esther?"

"Well, it's her return address and her stationery. Do you want me to open it?"

I'm confused. Why would there be a letter from Esther now and when would she have written it? "Yes, please."

I listen to the rustling of paper on the other end. I can see Esther's monogrammed stationery in my mind's eye—a watermark of fine lines running across the off-blue grain.

"It's dated February eighteenth," Vera says.

"That's the day after she left Manhattan. She must have been on the train home. Do you mind reading it to me?"

"Not at all."

Dear Bencke,

I'm sitting here in my compartment with my Saks hatbox on the seat beside me and thinking of our visit. It's always such a pleasure for me to see that age does not diminish you. You haven't lost your looks, your passion, your voice. You are as you were from the moment you bellowed your way into the world, a force to be reckoned with. I had a wonderful time with you, Bencke. Our visits, rare as they are, are a highlight of my life now and I so look forward to them. I hope that doesn't sound pathetic to you with all your causes and interests and fascinating friends.

"Do you want me to continue?"
"Please."

I probably should have told you this while I was visiting, Bencke, but I was embarrassed, so here goes. I've met a man. At this age if you can imagine. He's a professor emeritus at the university, in the science department. Spiders are his specialty and he's often "in the field" as he calls it, when a significant new or old species is discovered. He's found a rare jumping spider in the forests of Borneo where he's been for almost a month. It's actually very interesting. His name is Jim. I hope you'll meet him one day soon.

I can hear the water dripping into the tub from my jacket.

"It doesn't sound like she was ready to kill herself, does it?" I ask Vera. "She sounds so happy!"

"I don't know what to say, Anna. It doesn't sound like it. Would it help if I came there? I can get time off work and be there in three days."

"No, Vera. I hope to leave soon. But I love you for even offering."

"The offer holds if you need it. Have you talked to the witnesses?" she asks.

"Inspector McHugh took me to see one but refused to take me to the other one. I'm going to go on my own. I got his name from the first witness and I'm going to visit Louise, Esther's maid. She might know something."

"There's something else," Vera says, a catch in her voice.

"What?" I almost don't want to know.

"Ida Idestam died."

"Oh no, not Ida."

"There was an obituary in the *Times* yesterday. She was eighty-seven. Had a heart attack in her sleep. The funeral is Thursday and I wouldn't have mentioned it, but I thought you might like me to send flowers or something."

* * *

I met Ida Idestam at my first interview with the California Perfume Company. I had just left Weiner and Son and moved to a rooming house on West Twenty-Fifth. I was looking for work and the newsie on the corner was letting me look through his papers every morning. I was thrilled when I saw that the California Perfume Company was looking for depot managers. I knew a little about the company; it sold creams and lotions and household cleaning products door-to-door. I could be my own boss, work my own hours, and make a lot of money. I had read about one depot manager who made over a thousand dollars in six months.

April 12, the day of my interview, dawned providentially. It had been raining for almost a week but cleared up as I was leaving the house.

I had hoped to wear my lavender traveling suit for the interview. It was the only decent piece of clothing I had left, but I burned the hem trying to spot-clean it with solvent the night before, so I made do with my best factory outfit—a second-hand pin-striped black-and-white walking skirt and a high-necked white blouse. My one hat was wilted beyond repair, so I tied my hair back with a red and orange striped scarf in what I hoped was a jaunty manner and put on dangly black fake opal earrings.

The California Perfume Company office was on Chambers Street in downtown Manhattan. The building was modern and well cared for, with mirrors on the lobby walls and elevator panels. I expected the office to be just as chic, with a comfortable reception area, so when I opened the outside door I was surprised that I had walked right into the main office where two women and one man were working at desks. Embarrassed that I hadn't knocked, I started to back out. One of the women, Ida it turned out, smiled at me and came over. She was the shortest woman I have ever seen and took quick, tiny steps, leaning forward from the waist, like she was perpetually in a rush.

Ida put her hand on my elbow and guided me over to a broad oak desk where David McConnell, the president of the company, was sitting. I recognized him from pictures in the newspaper. He was reading something on his desk and stroking his chin. He didn't look up.

"Miss Grieve is here, Mr. McConnell," Ida said. "Your eleven o'clock?" She turned and winked at me.

Without looking up, Mr. McConnell told Ida to tell me to take a seat. Ida pulled out the chair in front of his desk, winked at me again, and went back to her desk.

The chair was wobbly and I had to position my feet hip width apart to keep it steady. I felt like a fool sitting there in my second-hand clothes with my legs apart.

"You're young, Miss Grieve," Mr. McConnell said when he finally looked up. He looked older than his pictures. His face was heavier and his hairline was receding, but he had the same dark handlebar mustache and penetrating eyes. "From your letter I expected someone older."

"With respect, Mr. McConnell, I'm the same age you were when you started the California Perfume Company."

"Are you now?" He smiled and glanced down at the letter on his desk. "Your letter says you want to be a depot manager with us."

"I do," I said, "very much."

"How did you hear about the California Perfume Company?"

"I've read about your company, and about you, sir, in the *New York Times*."

"So you read the *Times*, do you?"

"Yes. I also read *Atlantic Monthly, Harper's*—"

He put his hand out to stop me. "I think I understand, Miss Grieve. You're well read." I could see his lips turning up under his mustache.

"From what I've read, sir," I said, launching into the speech I'd been rehearsing all week, "your business is doing extremely well. It was brilliant of you to recognize the opportunity in selling beauty and household products to housebound women. I think I could be an asset."

"Surely you're not housebound, Miss Grieve."

"I'm not housebound, no sir."

He sat looking at me for a few moments. The two secretaries went on clicking at their typewriters as though no one else was in the room.

"Tell me about your family, Miss Grieve," he said. "What do they think of your wanting to become a depot manager for the California Perfume Company?"

"I have no family to speak of."

"Let me be blunt, Miss Grieve," he said, folding his hands on top of the desk. His nails were beautifully manicured. "You don't look like you would be interested in the products we sell. Not that you aren't attractive in a bohemian kind of way. Your height and carriage give you stature and elegance, but my business is based on a more traditional view of womanhood."

"I grew up within the confines of that view, Mr. McConnell. All I would have to do is change the way I dress and wear a little lip rouge."

"And you'd be willing to do that?"

"I'm willing to do whatever it takes to make my life work in Manhattan."

Ida got up from her desk when the interview was over, stepped out into the hall with me, and closed the door behind her. "My dear," she said, pressing an envelope into my hand, "get yourself nicely dressed for your next interview. Don't go to Saks or Macy's. Right behind Gimbels, a little to the south and down a few steps, there's an Italian tailor named Leo. He'll make you something wonderful for a fraction of the price. I've made your next appointment with Mr. McConnell in ten days so Leo will have time to fit you properly."

I returned ten days later in a ruby red hip-length jacket nipped in at the waist, the ruffles of a cream blouse peeking out at my throat. My skirt was straight, mid-calf, aubergine, with a double kick pleat at the back. I'd spent part of Ida's money on a hairdresser that morning and my hair was swept back from my face and up in a smooth, bouffant chignon. I'd bought a hat for the occasion, a black velvet tam-o'-shanter with a cut steel brooch on one side, but I was so proud of my hair, I decided not to cover it up. Ida beamed at me when I walked in.

We never became close friends, Ida and I, but she became an important part of my life and I think I became an important part of hers. As far as I know, she had never married or had children. Fourteen times in my forty years with the California Perfume Company, I was named highest-selling depot manager of the month, and Ida was at each awards ceremony. In 1916, when I won a Ford Runabout for having the highest sales for the past five years, Ida was the first person I drove through the streets of Manhattan.

I can still see her sitting beside me as I honked my way through the traffic with the best of them, one hand on her hat, the other over her mouth, laughing with delight. When I bought the house on West Twenty-Fifth, Ida came to my housewarming. She brought a white orchid in a white jardinière and a bottle of champagne. She didn't stay long, but she was there.

In 1939, when the California Perfume Company had changed its name, Ida and I went to the celebratory dinner. We had both retired by then. Ida was shorter and bent but hadn't lost an ounce of her vitality. We sat at a large round table with some of the other people we knew, all of us wearing big white buttons with "Avon" slashed across them in hot pink and black.

* * *

"I almost didn't recognize you," Mr. McConnell said when I returned for my second interview. "Sit down, my dear."

Thirty minutes later, I walked out of the office with a contract in my purse and the California Perfume Company Manual of Instruction under my arm. For seventy-five cents I had become the youngest depot agent the California Perfume Company had ever hired.

"If you conduct your business the way you conducted yourself during our interviews," Mr. McConnell said, "I have no doubt that you will be a great success."

• CHAPTER FOURTEEN •

Inspector McHugh closes his office door, sits down behind his desk, and tells me to sit down.

Before I'm even seated, he barks, "What exactly do you think you're doing?"

"What do you mean?" I ask, wondering how he found out what I had done.

"You know perfectly well what I mean. You went to see your sister's maid. You went to see the other witness. You're interfering with our work."

"How do you know I saw them?"

"They called me. That's how I know. You frightened Louise and made Mr. Kaldas angrier than he usually is."

"I'm just trying to get to the bottom of what really happened."

"What is it you think we're doing?"

"But you haven't told me anything new," I say, controlling my rising anger.

He looks away for a few moments and drums his fingers on the desk. "I don't report to you," he says, looking back at me. "I report to my superiors. If you have any other plans for doing your own detective work, I'd like you to tell me about them."

I'm still standing, my hand on the back of the chair. "Is there anything else?"

"Nothing."

Resisting the impulse to slam the door as I leave, I walk down the hall thinking about how often I've provoked this kind of reaction in the past. Nathaniel used to get impatient with my stubbornness and Jack, my first romantic attachment in Manhattan, said I was a bully.

* * *

I met Jack the same day the California Perfume Company hired me, and for the longest time I considered that day—April 22—my lucky day.

Immediately after I was hired, I went home to make a coffee to take upstairs to study the new manual. There was a man at the kitchen counter with his back to me. I sat down at the heavy, rectangular table to wait my turn and started flipping through the manual. It was impressive. It explained how to canvass, when to canvass, how to get customers interested in new products, the best time to make deliveries, how to send in an order, how to retain credit with the company, and most importantly how to make three hundred dollars a year working half time. I intended to do better than that.

When the man said hello, I looked up and gasped. I had seen him often at the Lafayette library when I was pregnant. He usually arrived shortly after I did. He would stop at the doorway of the reading room when he arrived, take off his brown fedora, unbutton his long camel-hair coat, and make his way to the north end of the room, where they kept the newspapers. He would select one and take it to the bank of wing chairs along the south wall. His routine was always the same. He would put his hat on one chair and set the newspaper on a chair beside it. His coat would go on a third chair beside the newspaper. Then he would unbutton his jacket, lift the newspaper from the middle chair, sit down, cross his legs, sharpen the crease in his trousers, and his face would disappear behind the newspaper. He stayed like that for thirty or forty minutes, his very shiny shoes shifting every now and then. I thought then—and I still do—that he was the most elegant man I'd ever seen.

* * *

"I'm Jack Griffin," he said that day in the kitchen. "Second floor, first room on the right."

Given that he was right across from me, I wondered why we hadn't met before. "I'm Anna Grieve. I just moved in. Second floor, first room on the left."

"Sorry we haven't met," he said, answering my unspoken question. "I just got back from Chicago. Can I make you a coffee and tell you about life at 201 West Twenty-Fifth?"

Coffee in front of us, he began. "Starting at the third floor attic, we have Melanie, the would-be ballerina. She walks dogs to help pay the rent. On our floor, we have Steve, a would-be chef who works as a stevedore to keep himself in loose change. Then there's Lily, the would-be actress and you and me. The main floor is a common area. Kitchen, two bathrooms, storage. The cast of characters changes often. I've been here longest and I have no complaints. I rarely see the other people. No one touches my food shelf and there's almost never a dirty cup in the sink."

Jack was right. I so rarely saw the other tenants, it felt like we had the place to ourselves.

"And you're a would-be what?" I asked him that day.

"Oh that's easy. I'm a would-be painter, and you?"

I thought for a moment. "I'm a would-be would-be."

He laughed.

I was surprised at first that Jack wanted to spend time with me. He was older, handsome, an artist. And he obviously had money. The first time he took me out, I told him that I would start treating him as soon as I could afford it. Jack said he found both me and my offer charming.

Jack was the sales representative for a Chicago pharmaceutical firm promoting a German amphetamine that claimed to cured asthma, narcolepsy, and depression. He traveled across the United States selling it to doctors. I asked him once if it worked and he said he really didn't know, but he didn't think it did any harm.

When he was home, Jack put on a big black smock and painted. Because his room smelled of paint and mineral spirits, he kept the window open to keep the smell down, but it never bothered me. I would sit back on his bed and watch him spread and layer and dab with colors whose names were as thrilling to me as the hues themselves: ultramarine and burnt umber and alizarin crimson and cobalt blue. When he was done, he would soak a rag with oil of spike lavender and methodically rub the paint from his hands in a circular fashion. He would then soak an orangewood stick in the oil and clean under his nails. Once a week, he had a professional manicure.

I loved Jack's work. It was primitive and vivid with wild, indecipherable shapes. He took me to a museum on Third Street shortly after we met to show me what he was trying to do. Fauvism, he called it, like Matisse and Derain. He did a portrait of me once in that style. With my full lips and wild hair, he made me look like Medusa, but there was no doubt that it was me.

I don't know if I loved Jack but I loved the idea of him. We would stride through the city, my arm through his, our long coats swinging with our perfectly matched long strides. He came shopping with me to choose new business clothes, took me to lectures on theology and metaphysics, to The Klatch on Washington for espresso, to Jamie's Bar on Broadway for martinis. Jack loved being my teacher. And I soaked it up.

One evening about eight months after I had moved in, we took a trip to Coney Island. We had just finished dinner and I had a yen for cotton candy. It was October, and becoming cool. By the time we got there, the wind had picked up and the waterways around the island made it feel colder and damp. To make things worse, the food carts were closed. It was close to eleven when we started home and Jack was in a bad mood.

"I still can't believe you don't know what happened to your parents," he said sulkily on the ferry walk. "Why they never came over, why they never wrote."

"I've told you. The Count and Countess didn't talk about it."

"I can't believe you didn't ask."

"I did at first. I've told you that too. I stopped after a while. Everyone pretended that nothing was amiss. We didn't talk about unpleasant things."

"But how could they adopt you? Wouldn't they have to have either your parents' approval or evidence that you'd been abandoned?"

"I don't know, Jack," I sighed, tired of going through it again.

"Did you never talk with Esther about all of this?"

"Of course I did. It's hard to explain Esther, Jack. She doesn't remember a lot of things and when you press her, she gets afraid and withdraws. You have to know her to understand. She's small and fragile and makes everybody feel like they're the most important person in the world. Everybody wants to take care of her."

"That's a powerful aphrodisiac," he said.

I kicked him.

"Sounds like you're jealous." He laughed and kissed me on the head. He held me close on the walk home but as usual, once we were alone, he made sure there was a safe distance between us. I had decided that morning to finally do something about it.

Reaching into the cupboard for cups, Jack asked me if I wanted coffee or tea.

Nervous but determined, I put my arms around his waist from behind. "What I want is for you to make love to me."

* * *

After getting a few doors closed in my face, I had found an almost perfect way to get potential customers to invite me and my California Perfume Company products into their homes. When I got to the door, before I rang the bell, I opened my case, held it out in front me, and *then* knocked or rang so whoever answered saw rows of gleaming bottles and jars nestled in highly polished mahogany partitions before they saw anything else. It almost always worked.

Even so, I had a few rejections. Once by an elderly women in a pink chenille housecoat with a cigarette hanging out of her mouth who opened her door, looked over my case, and closed the door without saying a word. Another time, a boy of about ten yelled back into the house, "Ma! There's a tall lady at the door with a big box!"

"Tell her I'm not home, Jeffrey," his mother yelled back, "and tell her that we have a dog."

The rest of the time, it was going very well.

* * *

Every night when I got home, I slipped off my shoes, hung my business clothes on the fire escape to air, and put on a pair of loose men's trousers and a man's white shirt. I then took a pair of fresh white cotton gloves from a box I kept on my closet floor and refreshed my sample case.

Sitting cross-legged on my bed with my case on one side and a lint-free white cloth on the other, I would remove each jar and bottle from the case, polish it with my gloves, and place it on the towel. I would then polish the case, inside and out, with a furniture polish made by my company and re-arrange the items so there was always something new to look at.

"What do you think of my replacing the Lait Virginal Milk Bath with the Sweet Sixteen Face Powder?" I asked Jack one evening. He was sitting across from me reading the newspaper. "I haven't replaced it for about six weeks."

He came over and reached for the Lait Virginal.

"No. Don't touch it, Jack. I've just polished everything."

"Sorry." He stepped back. "I think you should keep the Lait Virginal."

"Why?"

"Because every woman wants to be a virgin."

"Really?" I asked, wondering if he thought less of me now that we were lovers.

"Change it if you want to, Anna, and change your clothes. Why do you insist on putting on men's clothes as soon as you get home? You dress better for your customers than you do for me." That was another of his pet peeves. "You look so much more feminine in skirts and nice shoes. These clothes make you look like a man."

"Jack," I said, pulling him close and resting my head on his chest, "you're old fashioned. But you know, I think you're right. I'll stick with the Lait Virginal for another few weeks. Everybody does seem to love it."

• CHAPTER FIFTEEN •

J ack greeted me at the door with an envelope in his hand.

"I think it's from your sister," he said.

My heart leapt at the sight of her neat hand. I hadn't seen Esther since I'd left Winnipeg three years earlier and our correspondence had become spotty.

Dear Bencke, the letter began. After a little small talk, she got to the point. She needed an abortion and hoped I could find her someone to do it in Manhattan so Charles would never find out that she was pregnant or what she had done.

"Let her take a taxi," Jack said to me when I told him. "You're arranging the trip, the abortion, the hotel. She's arriving after midnight. At least get a good night's sleep before this ordeal."

I might as well have met her at the station. I spent half the night she was to arrive worrying about her fighting her way through Grand Central and finding a cab. The other half of the night I lay awake wondering about whether I should try to persuade her not to have the abortion. I was still convinced she would make a wonderful mother and that motherhood would be good for her.

It was raining heavily when I left the house to meet her the next morning, so I grabbed an umbrella to walk the few feet to the brothel just down the street. They had a doctor on the third floor who was sympathetic to the female cause and wasn't afraid to break the law. I met with him after Esther's letter came and felt she would be in good hands.

As I waited under my umbrella by the steps of the brothel, the rain pelted so heavily that it blocked out the traffic noises. I watched Esther's cab arrive. The driver came around and opened her door. She took his arm and stepped out, looking around for me. Esther looked so thin and frightened. I was tempted to ask if she wanted to go for a coffee and talk it over, but I decided it was her decision, not mine.

"Is this the place?" she asked looking up at the brownstone as we climbed the steps.

"Yes," I said, hoping she wouldn't notice that the door knocker was a naked woman with her arms above her head and her legs apart.

Earl answered the door. "Hello, Anna. Good to see you."

"You too, Earl."

Esther glanced at me briefly.

"Dr. Devlin is upstairs," Earl said. "He said to send you right up."

We parked our umbrellas in a brass stand and went up three flights of stairs, the last flight uncarpeted and narrower than the first two. I knocked on a low black door.

"Come in," a relaxed male voice said.

The doctor was standing at his desk, drying his hands on a white towel as we walked in. It was his hands in part that had convinced me that Esther was safe with him. They were large and well formed with square fingertips, the nails short and clean.

"Nice to see you, Miss Grieve," he said. "This must be your sister. How are you, Mrs. Kinnear? How far along are you?"

"Eight weeks."

"That's good. Have you brought the fee?"

Esther took an envelope out of her purse and gave it to him. Her hands were trembling. He put the envelope in his pocket without looking inside.

Trying to keep calm and look anywhere but at Esther, I focused on the room. It was small, hospital green, with a rain- and leaf-splattered dormer window that cast speckled light over the brown leather hospital gurney beneath it. A desk was wedged across one corner with a swivel chair in front of it. A white wood-framed screen stood in the opposite corner. A pile of folded white sheets sat on a small chest of drawers beside the screen. The doctor took a sheet from the pile and gave it to Esther.

"Please go behind that screen, Mrs. Kinnear, and remove your skirt and underlinens. Wrap yourself in this sheet and lie down on the gurney over there."

"What shall I do with my shoes?" Esther asked.

I looked at the doctor.

"Your shoes don't matter, Mrs. Kinnear," he said kindly. "Leave them on or take them off. If you're having second thoughts about the procedure, you can always make another appointment. You won't have that luxury if you go ahead."

I was glad he said what I had decided not to. It took all my will not to stop her as she went behind the screen.

When the procedure was over, Esther started crying. Wailing was the word I used later with Jack. I didn't introduce Esther to him on that trip. I didn't think it was appropriate. I spent three days with her in a room at the Redburn, a hotel for women. While she rested and drank beef tea, I picked up trinkets and theater programs so she could show Charles what a gay visit we had had. I didn't mention the abortion. Neither did she.

* * *

"How was it?" Jack asked me when I came home after seeing Esther off at the station.

"It was terrible," I said. "I don't think she wanted to have the abortion."

"Why do you think that?"

"Because," and I started to weep, "because when it was over she started wailing so loudly that Mrs. Smith came up and asked Dr. Devlin if he could keep her quiet. They could hear her in the rooms downstairs."

Jack put his arms around me.

"My poor little Bencke," he said, like he was talking to a young child. I had told him some time ago that Bencke was Esther's pet name for me, but he'd never used it before.

"Don't call me that," I shouted. "Nobody but Esther can call me that." I asked him to leave, closed my door, and stayed in bed for three days. Jack brought me tea and toast and left it at the door. I heard him at my door often, listening to hear whether I was all right. When I emerged, ratty and exhausted, he said he'd never seen me like that before.

* * *

Shortly after Esther's abortion, I added womb veils to my line of products. I didn't tell Jack and I didn't tell the California Perfume Company, although I suspect the company knew and tacitly approved.

I found a family-run company in Brooklyn that specialized in industrial hoses and made a nice little profit on the side selling womb veils illegally. They were reluctant at first to deal with me. They thought

I might be working for one of the groups that wanted to expose people like them, but I went back with my sample case, told them about my work, and they finally agreed.

I would wait until my fourth visit with my customers to bring up the topic of family planning. They were usually comfortable with me by then and I would accept the coffee that was always on offer and join my customer in her parlor. She would bring in the coffee and a plate of homemade cookies or cake and we would discuss the order I had just delivered and items in development and then I would casually ask about her family.

If she said she had children, I would feign awe at how she managed. She would explain or complain. I would then ask whether she had ever considered family limitation. There are only two answers to that question I've learned—"Having children is God's will" or "If only there were a way."

If the answer was God's will, I would turn the conversation back to the products. If the answer was "If only there were a way," my heart would leap and my hand would go into my handbag and bring out the blue velvet pouch with the powdered womb veil. I would pull apart the drawstring and take out the flesh-colored contraption, blow off any excess talcum, and hold it in my open palm, leaning over a little so she could look at it. I had learned over the years that I had to let them approach it, not the other way around. They were interested, all of them, all of the time, but most were a little hesitant at first.

I would then do what I came to call my flying womb veil trick. I would push the rubber sides of the womb veil together and we would watch it fly across the room. It always broke the ice. I would pick it up, blow off any dust that had collected, and offer it to her again, palm open. She was usually relaxed enough at that point to take it.

"It's just rubber," I would say. "You see how firm yet flexible it is? Once you insert it, you won't even know it's there and best of all, neither will your husband. It may not be one hundred percent reliable, but it has helped many women, myself included, prevent many pregnancies."

* * *

About six months after I started selling womb veils, I was delayed on the El and ran the few blocks to a customer's house. I arrived breathless. Mrs. Stone put her hand on my back and guided me into her drawing room where fourteen women stood up and clapped.

"Ladies," Mrs. Stone said, "this is our Miss Grieve. I hope you don't mind," she said to me, her hand still on my back, "I told my friends and neighbors about you. They would all like womb veils. And," she continued, "as not everyone could be here today, would it be possible to order six extras? A total of twenty?"

There was a note under my door when I got home. Jack had gone to Chicago and would see me in seven to ten days. I was annoyed that he had taken off again without telling me beforehand, but my overwhelming emotion was relief. I could go to Sachs's Café and stay as late as I liked without Jack sighing and looking at his watch. I could wear my men's clothes at home without feeling guilty. I was surprised at how much I looked forward to being on my own again.

• CHAPTER SIXTEEN •

The duty officer tells me that the inspector is in his office and I can go right in.

"It's open," he calls when I knock. He seems to be in a better frame of mind; he stands up when I enter and waits for me to sit down before he does.

"Have you decided what to do about the dog?" he asks. He doesn't seem angry anymore but I'm surprised he's asked me here to talk about Licorice.

"I have," I tell him.

* * *

I'd been to the kennel earlier that morning. It was on the outskirts of the city, too far for even me to walk, so I took a taxi and asked the driver to wait. There were signs advertising it all the way—Wagging Tails—so we couldn't miss it. We couldn't have missed it anyway. It was the only house for miles, a small clapboard bungalow in a large empty lot surrounded by a chain link fence. There were a few dogs in the lot when we arrived, but Licorice wasn't among them.

"I'm Mrs. Kinnear's sister," I said to the skinny, red-haired woman behind the counter. "I'm here to pick up Licorice."

She rummaged through a cardboard box of papers and took one out. "It doesn't say here that anyone but Mrs. Kinnear can pick him up."

"Oh," I said, loath to tell her that Esther was dead. Other than Vera, I hadn't told anyone and it felt like saying it to a stranger would make it true.

I went ahead, though. I had to start sooner or later. "Please call the police department if you don't believe me," I ended. "Inspector McHugh at the Ness Street Station. I have the number here."

Not bothering to take the number from me, she reached over and patted me on the arm. "I'm sorry to hear that," she said. "And we're sorry to see him go. He's such a trooper—he actually earns his keep. He's what we call a socializing dog. He calms the new boarders."

"Do you want to keep him?" I asked hopefully. Taking Licorice home was the last thing I wanted to do. It would feel like I was still looking after Esther.

"If you're comfortable with that, we'd love it. We'll even waive the kennel charge. Do you want to see him before you go?"

I didn't.

* * *

"Good," Inspector McHugh says when I tell him what had happened at the kennel. "Perfect timing. We're about to close the case."

I hadn't expected this. "Why?"

"Because we haven't found anything to suggest foul play."

"Have you found more journals?"

"No."

"Have you looked?"

"Not personally, but my officers have searched thoroughly. There's nothing to suggest anything but suicide."

"May I go through the house once more before you officially close things?"

"I thought you said that felt like you were invading her privacy."

"I think I could do it now."

"I can't let you do it now. Access is still restricted. My team will be going in one last time. It shouldn't take more than a day, two at the most. After that, I'll give you the key and you can do whatever you want."

"My concern is that you've missed something, Inspector."

"We don't usually miss things, Miss Grieve." I can tell I'm pushing him again.

"I'm sorry. I don't mean to suggest that, but you're all so sure it's a suicide, I'm afraid you're not seeing any other scenarios. I remembered just this morning that a man Esther's husband sent to jail made some threats on his life."

"Isn't her husband dead?"

"Yes."

"How many years ago were those threats made?"

"Just after the war."

"The Great War?"

"Yes."

He raises his eyebrows and shakes his head. "That was twenty-four years ago."

"Yes."

"And you think this man went to the train station to find his wife and pushed her under a train."

"Isn't it possible?"

He sighs. "Can you give me his name?"

"I don't have it."

"Miss Grieve. . . "

"I'm sorry," I say, realizing how desperate I sound. "I'm grasping at straws." My voice breaks. "I just don't want her to have killed herself."

He looks at me, the exasperation gone. "I understand."

After a few moments, he looks at his watch. "I'm sorry, Miss Grieve. I have a meeting. Would you like me to have one of my men to drive you back to the hotel?"

"Thank you. I'll walk. I need to clear my head."

I walk about a block and hail a cab. I ask the driver to take me to Glow's Hardware at Main and Aikens and to wait outside while I make some purchases and then take me on to 368 Wellington Crescent, Esther's house.

It's dusk when we turn onto her street. There are no sidewalks here, just broad roads and sweeping driveways turning off them, flanked by evergreens. The only people who walk in this neighborhood are the servants coming and going.

Concerned that a taxi at Esther's door might look suspicious to the neighbors, I ask the taxi driver to go past Esther's house before stopping. I pull my parka hood over my head and walk back to her place holding the bag from the hardware store close to my chest. The road is slippery. I look around when I get to the house to make sure no one is watching and walk to the front door. The restricted access sign is still there. Using the brick wall to steady myself so I don't slip and fall, I walk along the side of the house to Esther's study at the back. It's magical back here even in the winter. Large conifers in greens ranging from mint to almost black, white birch and black spruce, and tall bleached grasses. Big clay pots are turned over, lining a path to the pond. I put the bag down in front of the French doors at Esther's study and peer in. I don't know who I expect to be there. Charles is dead. Esther is dead. The servants are long gone and Licorice is safe at the kennel.

I take a leather glove and a hammer out of the bag, put the glove on, look over my shoulder, and bring the hammer down on the glass just above the door handle. I pick out the shards of glass, pile them to the side of the door, and ease my gloved hand in to open the deadbolt imagining a conversation with the inspector.

"Really?" I would say when he tells me that someone has broken into Esther's house. "Maybe someone noticed that the house was empty. Was anything taken?"

I wonder if I should take something to make it look like a real burglary.

I stop inside the doorway. Should I take my boots off? Would a real burglar take his boots off? I decide to leave them on.

The room doesn't look much different than it did when I was there a few days ago. The magazines on a side table are a little neater perhaps.

I walk over to the floor-to-ceiling teak-fronted bookcase that lines an entire wall. I run my hand along the books on the shelves. Framed pictures are standing in front of some of the books—Esther and Charles at the wedding I missed because I was pregnant; the Count and Countess when they were married in Russia; Licorice I, Licorice II and the latest, Licorice III, one looking exactly like the other. There's a picture of me when I was about eleven in my egg boy's clothes, feet apart, hands on my hips, squinting into the sun.

I move along the bookcase. There's a section on dog breeding and care, another on mineral and biodynamic farming. Esther and the Countess believed that chemicals stripped the soil and destroyed the nutrition in food. It was the only thing I had ever known Esther to be adamant about. She refused to have pasteurized milk in the house.

There are several shelves with the children's books she collected for the library, stacks of women's magazines going back to 1899—*McClure's, Women's Way, Redbook*. I'm surprised at the impressive collection of political and historical books: *The International Jew, the World's Foremost Problem* by Henry Ford, *The Protocols of the Elders of Zion, Mein Kampf* by Adolph Hitler. I pull it out. It's in German. I didn't know that Esther could read German. I also didn't know that she was interested in mental health but there are at least a dozen books on psychiatry with *A History of Neuroscience* in front of a low shelf, open to a page on the benefits of electro-convulsive therapy.

A sheet of paper with writing in Esther's hand is tucked in the margin: *fast eight to twelve hours before sessions, water only. Some scalp shaving may be necessary. Complications could include memory loss and headaches.*

I didn't know Esther was interested in electro-convulsive therapy. I don't know whether she actually went through with it, and if she did, whether it helped.

I spend close to an hour in the study. I take down books and peer behind them. I pull over a stool to reach the top shelves. I take the stool to the two closets and do the same thing.

When I get to the hall, I take my boots off. Burglar or not, the carpets are off-white and I can't bear to dirty them.

Everything is cream and white in Esther's bedroom—the bedspread, the curtains, the French Victorian furniture. Even the little pillow on the floor where Licorice sleeps. There's a breathtaking view of the back garden from the floor-to-ceiling windows on the east wall.

I go through her closets, all four of them. I open every hatbox, look in every handbag and inside every shoe. I get down on my knees and up on my toes and peer and feel into corners. I look under the bed and in bathroom drawers. I hit my head at one point on a corner shelf and start to weep. I don't know what I'm looking for. Clues, I guess. Something to give to the police so they won't close the case yet. Something to absolve my guilt.

I pull open the top drawer of Esther's bedside table. There's a piece of navy velvet with a hatpin in it. Behind it are bundles of letters tied with blue ribbon. I undo one of the ribbons and open a few letters. They're from Charles when they were courting. So many letters.

The compartment below the drawer is locked. I try to open it with my fingernail and then the hatpin. When it won't open, I use the claw end of the hammer and ruin the finish. There are a few more letters from Charles and a large envelope in the Countess's handwriting with Esther's name on it and mine.

• CHAPTER SEVENTEEN •

Everything fell apart for Jack and me one warm March weekend a year after Esther had her abortion. I think we both knew it was coming.

It was a Friday morning and I had a lot of deliveries to make.

"Where do you think you're going?" Jack asked, pulling me back as I was trying to get out of bed without waking him. "It's not even six."

"I thought you were still sleeping," I said.

"No such luck," he said, nuzzling my back with his face.

An hour and a half later, I ran down the stairs, shopping bags filled with my deliveries for that day slapping against my hips, worrying that I would never get it all done. My first stop was the brothel down the street where I had a monthly standing order—perfumes, powders, bath salts, body creams, and of course womb veils to prevent the natural consequences of all that seduction.

Jack was shocked when I told him the brothel was a customer, horrified when I told him how I found out about it in the first place.

* * *

I was working for Weiner and Son at the time. By the time I had paid my rent and put away the few cents each week that I promised myself I would, I couldn't even afford a coffee at Sachs. I wondered how my roommates Freya and DeeDee, who also worked in the garment factories, could afford such beautiful dresses and jewelry. When I asked, they told me they made "a little extra" at Mrs. Smith's on West Twenty-Fifth. They made it sound like there was nothing to it. "You wear nice clothes and sit on their laps and sometimes that's all they want," Freya said.

"What if they want more?" I asked.

"Then you take off your nice clothes and sit on their laps," DeeDee said, and they both fell over on the bed laughing. "They don't hurt you. It's all very hoity-toity. Government officials and businessmen. They can't even get in the door without a reference. Anyone misbehaves, there's Earl to deal with."

Twirling around to show off her new green silk skirt, she said, "And we get to keep these. Mrs. Smith buys her girls new clothes every few months. The men like a change."

I knew what they were talking about, of course, but for a few minutes, sitting on somebody's lap and getting paid for it seemed preferable to living the way I was or dipping into the Count's bank account.

So I brushed off my lavender suit and walked over to West Twenty-Fifth on a chilly Sunday in March. DeeDee had set up a meeting for me with Mrs. Smith.

The house was in Chelsea—the area I live in now, one of the few I had somehow missed in my earlier wanderings. It was an upscale residential area on the West Side. The homes were very posh: five stories, stained glass bay windows. I was surprised to see room for rent signs in some of the windows. When I reached the brothel, I was so nervous, I walked by four times before the sky cracked open and forced me to go up the stairs and lift the unusual brass knocker.

"I have an appointment with Mrs. Smith," I said to the large colored man who answered the door. It was Earl, of course, not quite as beefy then, with a black patch over one eye that he wore, he told me later, when he needed to look more menacing. He was in his bouncer's uniform—tight black pants and a navy double-breasted jacket with big bronze buttons that I tried not to stare at. Each one was a pornographic carving: an engorged penis, a breast with pursed lips around the nipple, a woman's rump with a finger going into an orifice.

"Unusual, aren't they?" Earl said, running his fingers over the penis. "Mrs. Smith has them imported from London. Do you have a card, Miss?"

"I don't," I said, embarrassed at being cardless.

"Don't worry about it," he said. "Mrs. Smith will fix you up with cards soon enough. She takes good care of her girls."

"She hired me on the spot," I told Jack, "but two days before I was to start, I knew I couldn't go through with it. Mrs. Smith was very gracious. She said she understood that this life wasn't for everyone; that I could come back if I changed my mind."

Jack sat listening to me, stony-faced.

"She's not what you think, Jack," I went on, regretting that I had even started. "She was born into a wealthy Washington family. She grew up with four brothers and her parents let her run freely with them until she was about fourteen when they started grooming her for marriage. When she was sixteen, they married her off to an older man who expected her to take over where his dead wife had left off. Six months later she ran away and came to New York. On her own. Imagine the courage, Jack. Her parents were too embarrassed to look for her. Her husband was too angry. She did what she had to do to stay alive. One of her clients—he's still a client—set her up in the brothel."

Jack sat looking at his hands in his lap, his lips tight.

"Aw, Jack," I said, going over to him and kneeling in front of his chair. "She's a moral woman. She keeps a clean house. Her girls are disease-free. She supports a hostel for indigent women and an orphanage. Her clients are some of the wealthiest men in New York."

"Enough, Anna," Jack said, getting up and going to my door. "I don't know how you could have even considered it and I don't want to hear anymore."

I didn't tell him when I started selling womb veils.

* * *

I was running down the stairs with my packages that Friday morning, worried that my time in bed with Jack would make my deliveries impossible, when a telegraph boy on a bicycle called out to me.

"Do you live there?"

"Yes," I said, not slowing my pace.

"You wouldn't happen to be Anna Grieve, would you?" he asked, walking his bike along the street with me at that point.

"Yes."

"Oh good, saves me a trip. I have a telegram for you, Miss. Please sign here."

COUNTESS ILL. ESTHER NOT COPING. COME SOONEST. CHARLES.

I put the telegram in my pocket.

I was surprised to see a police cruiser in front of the brothel and two uniformed officers standing at the stairs, legs apart, hands clasped behind their backs. The police were rarely needed at Mrs. Smith's and when they were, they were usually discreet about their presence.

"Are you Anna Grieve?" one of them asked as I tried to slip between them to go up the stairs.

"Yes."

"Please come with us, Miss," he said, taking my arm. "You're under arrest for violating the Comstock Act."

I was peeved. I'd been arrested twice before for distributing birth control pamphlets on the street and the routine was always the same. I was taken to the Mulberry station, given a stern talking-to by one of the inspectors, and sent home to mend my ways. Today, they were going to make me very late.

Instead of taking me to the Mulberry station this time, they drove to the new City Prison in lower Manhattan. I had watched the chateau-like building going up and as frightened as I was, I was interested in seeing if it was as grand inside as it was out.

I never found out. They took me straight to the basement, along a narrow hall that smelled of rot and ammonia and locked me in a tiny cell with one barred window near the ceiling where I could see people's feet going by. I gave them Jack's name and the address at the house and waited.

It was Friday. Jack showed up Monday afternoon.

"Are you all right?" he asked when we were out on the street, my bags on his arm.

"There were mice," I said. "At least I hope they were mice. I was afraid to lie down in case they crawled on me. I got one cup of coffee in the morning and a stale tomato sandwich at night. The bathroom was one big room with toilets and no sinks. No dividers or private stalls. I need a shower and maybe a delousing and I have to get to Winnipeg as soon as possible. The Countess is ill and Esther isn't coping well."

"I need to talk with you, Anna."

I could tell from his voice that something was wrong. "Why couldn't I reach you this weekend, Jack?"

"I was in Chicago. I told you I was going."

"You didn't."

"I thought I had." He stopped and put my packages down. He looked upset.

"When I got to Chicago Friday night," he said, searching my face for a reaction, "my wife, Rita, confronted me. She knows about us."

"Your wife?" I asked.

"Yes."

"You're married?"

"Yes."

"Since when?"

"Since before you knew me."

"Why did you never tell me?"

"You made it impossible to tell you."

"How could *I* make it impossible for you to tell me that you're married?" I said, trying not to raise my voice. People were going around us, annoyed at having to avoid the bags on the sidewalk, ignoring what was obviously becoming a heated conversation.

"Anna, you claim you want to hear the truth, but you don't really. You don't like it when I disagree with you. You get aggressive if I try and defend myself. So I've started to keep things to myself. To keep the peace. I honestly thought it wouldn't make a difference to you whether I was married or not. You don't seem to want children or commitment, so it seemed simplest to go on as we were."

"I may not want children or commitment, Jack," I said, "but I do want to be able to believe that you are what you present to me. How can I ever trust you again?"

Jack laughed out loud. "How can *you* ever trust *me*, Anna? You're selling womb veils illegally. God knows what else you haven't told me and you're asking how you can trust *me*?"

* * *

The porter lifted my suitcase into the rack above my bunk, told me dinner would be served in the dining car between five and seven-thirty, and wished me a good trip. Despite the events of the past few days, it was a good journey. The prairies calmed me, as they always do. The sun shone for the most part, melting what was left of the March snow, revealing bales of straw piled high, marking where one farm ended and another began.

I thought about Jack, how reluctant he had been to make love to me for so long, how little he had told me about his life. I'd wondered why he never took me with him on his trips, why he never told me how to reach him in an emergency. Now I knew. Perhaps he had children as well.

"I love you, Anna," Jack said to me before I left. "I'm moving back to Chicago, but I'll divorce Rita and come back here and marry you if you want me to."

If you want me to.

Halfway through the trip I had a dream that I've never forgotten. Vera calls it a reckoning dream; *rasplata* in Russian. She says they're the universe trying to show you your true path.

I'm running down the back stairs of a tall building. I have no idea where the building is or what I'm running from. I just know I have to get away. I reach the main floor and fling open the door and there in front of me is everybody I have ever known—Mamma and Pappa, Esther and Charles, the Count and Countess, the servants, Nathaniel and his parents and grandparents, the people from Weiner and Son, the people from the California Perfume Company, Vera, Jack, Earl, the girls from Mrs. Smith's, Moses, Simon from Sachs. They have their arms stretched out to me, all wanting something.

The train stopped in Sudbury the next morning, a mining town about a thousand miles from Winnipeg. I took my luggage and got off. I sent Charles a telegram telling him that I could not come to Winnipeg, bought a ticket back to Manhattan for the next morning, and booked into a hotel for the night.

Another telegram from Charles arrived two days after I got back home. The Countess had died and they were going ahead with the funeral without me. I was relieved.

• CHAPTER EIGHTEEN •

I lean back against Esther's bed, the envelope with our names on my lap. It's getting dark. I close the drapes and turn on Esther's lamp and pull out a lined sheet of paper with the Countess's writing. It's not dated.

My Dears, Esther and Anna,
When your mother asked the Count and me to take you to Winnipeg with us so many years ago, we agreed. I think you know that your mother and I were close, and there isn't much I would have refused her. She said that while your travel papers could be approved immediately with our sponsorship, there was a bureaucratic holdup with her papers and your pappa's that might take a few months to sort out. She wanted you out of harm's way as soon as possible, she said, which the Count and I understood. We weren't in any danger, but we wanted to escape the reactionary regime as well. We took you with us, expecting your parents to show up relatively quickly. We had paid for their passage and given them money for the trip.
We spent the first months here writing to them, expecting to hear back, not concerned. Overseas mail has always been spotty. At some point

our expectations turned to worry and then despair. We hired private detectives three times over the years with no success. Your parents seem to have disappeared.

We wondered how to tell you, what to tell you, when to tell you. The longer we hesitated, the easier it became to ignore the whole issue. We consoled ourselves with the fact that you girls did seem to be finding your own, very different, paths.

I've re-written this letter so many times, trying to find the best way to tell you all this, but it will probably sit in my desk drawer until I die, a testament to my fear of inflicting more pain on you, my inability to deal with things and my hope that a miracle will occur and your parents will simply one day appear.

Please forgive us if we did the wrong thing. What we did, we did out of love. I know we can never replace your parents, but over the years, the Count and I have come to love you as our own.

I turn off the light and pull back the drapes. A light snow is starting to fall, the flakes disappearing before they reach the ground. I wonder for a moment how they're managing to melt on the letter in my hand before I realize it's my tears. I climb onto Esther's bed and pull my knees to my chest. I can't remember ever feeling so empty. I sleep for about twenty minutes and lie there for another ten.

When I get up, I run my hand over the gash I've made in the bedside table trying to open it earlier and pull the cabinet door open to see if there's any veneer inside that could be affixed to the front. The cupboard feels about eight inches deep inside, but from the outside, I can see that it's a good foot deeper. I poke and shove at what I had thought was the end, and a panel collapses. There's a journal behind it. It begins on May 14, 1897.

We took Jeanne-Marie to the Ninette Sanatorium this morning. Dr. Ridout says she will get the rest and nutrition she needs there and could be home working in the kitchen within the year. But I could tell by the way he said it that she might not be home ever again. Charles and I will pay for her upkeep there, of course, and will employ her daughter, a timid, obedient girl of fifteen, as she has no relatives. I didn't tell Dr. Ridout that the only milk I allow in the house is unpasteurized. I still believe, despite the controversy over pasteurization and his strong views, that if you buy it from a reputable farmer, it does not cause tuberculosis. Many European experts on the subject agree with me but I must admit, I do wonder if I should stop teaching the women at the Sanctuary about the benefits of unpasteurized milk. I've been telling them that it's the perfect food and if they are not fortunate enough to have three well-balanced meals a day, which many of these women are not, they must have three glasses of unpasteurized milk.

How important the Ellis Street Sanctuary was to Esther. It was built shortly after I left Winnipeg, thanks mainly to the Countess's efforts. She started raising funds shortly before I left Winnipeg when I was pregnant. I suspect my pregnancy had something to do her sudden interest in the welfare of unwed mothers. It may have been her emotionally distant way of offering me support, although she certainly didn't suggest that I, like the other unwed mothers she was hoping to help, stay in Winnipeg to have the baby. I don't think she could have stood the personal and social repercussions.

I remember watching her rehearse her appeals with the Count before she actually went out. "This will be the only sanctuary open to all single pregnant women," she would say to him, pacing up and down his library, gesturing with her hands, convincing. Even I could see that. The Count would listen, pretending to be the entrepreneur and playing devil's advocate.

"But I believe we already have three homes for single compromised young women, my beautiful Countess Chernovski, do we not?"

"You're right of course, sir, we do," she would reply, ignoring his flirtation, "but the existing homes all have religious affiliations and I fear those affiliations and their accompanying moral attitudes keep many women from asking for the help they need. These are not bad girls," she would continue. "Many have come to Winnipeg to make better lives for themselves. They send most of what little money they earn back home. They are to be admired. They are brave young women on their own and it's not difficult to see how they would find comfort in a man's arms."

Almost the exact words Esther used the day I heard her talking to the volunteers at the Sanctuary so many years ago.

Esther became a volunteer when the Sanctuary opened. At first, she did whatever was asked of her. She took the infants on their daily outings in the three-seater carriages that Broughton Brothers, a Winnipeg carriage company, had designed and donated. She posted letters, sorted clothing donations, took notes at staff meetings.

When she and Charles married, she was promoted to working with the women one-on-one. She told me that she helped them understand that their children would be better off in a family with a mother and a father and financial security. She found them jobs as domestics and convinced two local secretarial schools to allocate four spaces each, free of charge, to teach them typing and shorthand. She wrote to me early on that she felt so proud and capable, doing something that mattered.

* * *

It's snowing heavily now and the sky above Esther's garden is gray with clouds threatening a blizzard. I put the journal and the letter into the paper bag with my hammer and glove and go down the stairs. My boots have left black puddles on Esther's pristine carpet. I slip the boots on and walk back to the hotel.

• CHAPTER NINETEEN •

When America finally entered the Great War, I was afraid that my California Perfume Company business would suffer. The country was already in a recession. But just the opposite happened. People couldn't afford expensive items so they perked themselves up with my powders and perfumes, anything to feel less deprived. I made enough in the first few years of the war to buy the house I'm still living in. I turned the top two floors into an apartment for myself and started renting the main floor out to people who needed it. I charged next to nothing, sometimes nothing at all.

I thought of Esther less often as the years went by and when I did, I didn't let myself go too deep. We exchanged letters. She told me she was fine. Busy at the Sanctuary. The Count was in good health. There was no mention of any problems with Charles.

So in February of 1918, four years after I'd visited her in Winnipeg, this letter came as a surprise.

I'm sorry to trouble you, Bencke, but I don't know where else to turn. Charles has contracted tuberculosis. It came out of nowhere and the doctor says he must go to a sanatorium. I cannot find one that allows

*families to live with the patients and I cannot be without Charles.
I think you know that. I'm hoping that you, who seem to be able to
accomplish anything, can find a place for us that will allow Licorice
and me to be with Charles during his confinement.*

* * *

I tried not to look shocked when the porter set Charles's wheelchair
on the platform at Grand Central Station a few weeks later. Esther
had told me he had deteriorated, but if she hadn't have been with him,
I wouldn't have recognized this frail old man with the lank hair as
Charles.

Trying to hide my dismay, I took the handles of the wheelchair
from the porter and walked it to the car talking, probably manically,
about the sanatorium. "You'll love the Goodenough Sanatorium. It's in
the Appalachians, acres of rolling hills with a lake in the middle of the
property. We should be there in just over an hour. They've put you in
Red Cottage. It's a little smaller than the others, but has the best view."

Esther followed behind, Licorice in a basket on her arm, his moist
nose resting on the rim.

* * *

"We call our program FAIRS," Dr. George Goodenough had said to
me on my first visit to the sanatorium. "Food, Air, Isolation, Rest,
and Support. We provide the first four, but only a loving family can
provide the fifth. We're the only sanatorium in the United States that
allows families to stay with their loved ones. I myself had tuberculosis,"
he said, knocking his chest proudly with his fist, "as did the two other
Goodenoughs who run the practice with me—my brothers Dennis

and Vaughan. We're all doctors and we're walking proof that what we do works."

The routine at Goodenough never varied. Every morning at seven, a fresh-faced nurse's aide in a starched white uniform arrived at Red Cottage carrying a small tray with two ounces of cod liver oil in a small glass, a thermometer in another glass, and a vase with a red carnation. She stood to one side as Esther's live-in nurse, Roberta Assuria, took Charles's temperature and recorded it on a chart.

When the aide left, Nurse Assuria sponged Charles down and dressed him in fresh pajamas. At eight, an orderly dressed in starched whites brought breakfast—pinhead oatmeal with full-fat cream and brown sugar; fried bread with maple syrup; and bacon and coffee with cream and sugar. All the meals were high fat to counteract the alarming weight loss that came with tuberculosis. Charles had gone from one hundred seventy-five pounds to one hundred seventeen.

After breakfast patients went to the lake. They walked if they could. They went by wheelchair if they couldn't. They were pushed in their beds if they couldn't sit up. The beds were adult-size cribs with wheels, not difficult to maneuver.

When Charles came back from the lake, Nurse Assuria took him out to the cure porch, an unheated addition to Red Cottage with wall-to-ceiling windows that remained open all year unless it was raining or snowing. Charles spent eight hours every day there in his bed on the cure porch, the theory being that complete inactivity and exposure to fresh air and sunlight were the best cures. He wasn't allowed to sit up in bed or read, although we could read to him.

I spent thirty-six weekends at the sanatorium with Charles and Esther. I usually left Manhattan on Saturday morning and drove back on Sunday night.

We would sit on the cure porch and watch the seasons pass: mist burning off from the valley below; the sky turning pink and blue and gray. We watched foliage go from green to burnt yellows to reds, saw the snow icing the evergreens melt away.

Did I want to be there? No, but I was glad I could help. I was relieved that Nurse Assuria was with us twenty-four hours a day to keep Esther reassured about Charles. From what I could see, she was handling the whole thing well.

* * *

My boyfriend at the time, a colored jazz pianist named Cedric, never stopped complaining about my weekend absences. I was missing his sessions at the Black and Blues Club. I was missing my flying lessons, but as much as I loved my time with Cedric, I loved even more the freedom of taking off in my Ford Runabout every Saturday morning: folding the top down, tying a kerchief over my hair, and letting her "fly low," as Cedric called it. It wasn't as thrilling as flying high, but it was good.

If it hadn't been for my Runabout, I would never have met Cedric. He was on duty at Saks valet parking one evening in November shortly after I won the car for outstanding performance with the California Perfume Company. He was leaning against a wall in uniform—black slacks and a white short-sleeved shirt—one foot crossed over the other, his hands in his pockets, a cigarette dangling from his lips.

"Very nice," he said, crushing the cigarette with his shoes. "Had any problems with the drive bands?" he asked, opening my car door and making sure I saw that he was taking in my legs. "They tend to fall out of adjustment in cold weather."

"Not yet. This one's brand new and we haven't been through a winter together yet."

"Well," he said, taking a card from the front pocket of his shirt and handing it to me, "if you have any problems, give me a call."

"Are you a mechanic?"

"No," he said. "But I know a lot about cars. I'm not a valet either. I'm here today to help out a friend. I'm a jazz musician—piano—and a pilot. I do champagne flights over Manhattan. If we could fit those long legs of yours behind the cockpit, you'd probably love flying."

Cedric took me up in his 1915 Curtis Jenny for the first time on a clear, cool Friday in June, just before sundown. He pulled a leather helmet over my hair and tightened the waistbelt of a brown, hip-length sheepskin jacket and gave me a pair of black leather gloves. "You look like you were born to fly, doll," he said as he helped me into the seat behind the cockpit. There was a small brown case on the floor at my feet. "The champagne is open," he yelled back at me from the cockpit. "Glasses are on the side. Help yourself and hand me the bottle of Coca-Cola. I don't drink when I'm flying."

What was it like to be in the air? It was an incredible mix of danger and freedom and possibility. The sky was deep purple and red; the retreating dome of the sun looked like it was on fire. Once my heart climbed back into my chest, it felt like it did when I grew wings in the root cellar in Podensk.

I shrieked when I looked down during that first flight and saw that we were higher than the sixty-story Woolworth building. Cedric, his white scarf flying out behind him, lifted his bottle in salute.

* * *

One day near the end of the eighth month of Charles's stay at the sanatorium, Dr. Goodenough asked Esther and me to join him in his office in the main house. We wondered why the doctor had asked us there. As far as we could see, Charles was holding his own. As we walked through the grounds, the leaves just starting to turn copper in the distance, I could see that Esther was nervous.

Dr. Goodenough's office was in the main house on the estate. Built around 1820 as a summer retreat for a wealthy Austrian couple, it had wide windows with dark green shutters and a wrap-around porch with four-seater swings on every side.

A secretary in a baggy purple dress ushered us into the doctor's office. The view was even better than ours from Red Cottage. Esther and I sat down in the two oak chairs facing Dr. Goodenough's desk. "Thank you for coming," he said. "Can I get you ladies a coffee or a lemonade?" We declined. "Good then, I'll get right to the point. Although Charles is not doing badly, he isn't recuperating as quickly as we had hoped. We'd like to perform a pneumothorax procedure."

The doctor glanced at me briefly as we both waited for Esther to say something.

"It's a fairly new technique," he went on after a few moments. "Perfected in Italy. It involves removing two of Charles's ribs and forcing nitrogen into one of his lungs with a needle. The nitrogen will collapse that lung and give it total rest."

Again, the doctor and I waited for Esther to say something.

"Does this kind of thing work?" I asked, wondering if Esther had perhaps gone into one of her states. She was sitting very erect in her chair, looking past Dr. Goodenough.

"I'll be honest with you," he said. "We have limited experience with the procedure here, but the overall success rates have been good. Do you have any questions?"

Still nothing from Esther.

"I'd like to give it a try," he said. "Mrs. Kinnear?"

Looking at him at last, she spoke quietly and calmly. "I'll talk with Charles about it."

The doctor glanced at me and then spoke to her. "Your husband is not well, Mrs. Kinnear. I'm not sure asking him is the best approach."

"I don't do anything without consulting Charles," she replied.

* * *

Two weeks after the operation, Charles was up five pounds. Nurse Assuria let him sit up in bed and read on his own for an hour a day. She started him on breathing exercises and let him walk, with her assistance, to the toilet. When he had put on another two pounds, she decided he could have a real bath.

What an occasion that was. Esther and I carried two dining room chairs to the bathroom and parked ourselves outside the door as Nurse Assuria walked him to the bathroom. She was a large woman, taller than me and strong; she probably weighed fifty pounds more than Charles did at this point. Esther and I sat there smiling, clasping each other's hands. When Charles turned and waved at us at the bathroom door, we laughed giddily.

Still holding hands, not speaking, we heard water filling the tub, then splashing. "Good," we heard Nurse Assuria say every so often. "Slowly, Charles. Slowly. Breathe. Good. Would you like more hot water?"

* * *

Once every weekend, I insisted that Esther walk the thirty minutes to the Princess Hotel in a nearby town just to get a break. When she balked, which she always did, I would remind her how much Charles liked their scones. She always acquiesced.

About a month after the operation Charles started to cough up blood. Esther was at the hotel when it happened. Nurse Assuria called the main house for the doctor and I stood outside Red Cottage waiting for Esther to return.

When Esther saw me, she dropped her bag of scones at the door and ran into Charles's room.

"It's under control, Mrs. Kinnear," Nurse Assuria said, coming out of Charles's room with Esther in front of her, her hand on Esther's back. "Why don't we go into the living room and wait a few moments. It will be better that way."

Nurse Assuria went to the sofa and sat down, patted the seat beside her for Esther to join her. "You have to know," she said, taking Esther's delicate hand in her own broad ones, "that despite this setback, Charles is doing well. He's put on seven pounds. His appetite has improved. I would like you to keep that in mind before you go in to see him again. He reads your face and your every movement. If you're worried, he'll worry, which won't help any of us."

Esther went to the front door and picked up the bag of scones she had dropped. She took them into the kitchen and came out a few moments later with a cut and buttered scone on a plate that she took into Charles.

"Would you like me to stay until tomorrow morning instead of leaving tonight?" I asked Esther later. She was shivering despite the fact that heat in the cottage was on.

"Please," she said, "if it's not too much trouble."

• CHAPTER TWENTY •

I left the sanatorium just after six the morning after Charles's attack and drove home through the beginning of a fall storm thinking about the people I'd met over the years who never became friends but had a permanent place in my heart.

Nurse Assuria had already become one of those people. She and Esther and I would often stay up and talk after Charles had turned in for the night. She couldn't hear enough about my life in Manhattan—the clubs and restaurants, my work with the California Perfume Company, my work with the birth control movement.

She herself had strong views on women and medicine. She loved being a nurse, but had always dreamed about being a women's doctor, so she and her husband, a high-school principal, decided one day that life was too short not to pursue her dream.

"We scrimped and saved for five years," she said. "It was fun. Like being students again. We rediscovered store windows and half-price movie matinees and libraries. We found a Greek restaurant that had such large portions we could get away with one meal between the two of us. Then Ralph, my husband, was diagnosed with colon cancer and we used the savings for his medical care."

"Is he all right?" I asked tentatively.

"No," she said matter-of-factly. "It was quite advanced by the time we discovered it. He died quickly. But I love my work here. I have nothing but compassion and respect for people like Charles and Esther."

Earl from the brothel down the street was in my heart as well. An understanding had passed between us the day I applied to work at the brothel and again when I came back a few days later to tell Mrs. Smith I couldn't work for her. An odd combination of toughness and grace, Earl patted me on the back then and told me not to worry about it. "If it's not the life for you, it's not. Things will work out as they were meant to."

When I bought my house, Earl came over with a box of Almond Roca, a pink ribbon tied around it. Refusing to come in for a glass of champagne, he stood at the door and wished me luck. Told me the girls said I would love the Almond Roca.

I remember years ago looking out my office window and seeing him, squatting in the road, his black pants taut over his rump as he slid a piece of cardboard under a nestling that must have fallen out of a tree. He stood up with the naked creature balanced on the cardboard when two adult birds appeared out of nowhere. They dive-bombed his head, then flew off, one retreating and one advancing, going for his eyes. He put the cardboard on the sidewalk and ran into the house with his hands over his head.

* * *

By the time I got back to the city from the sanatorium that Monday morning, the rain that had been falling lightly and steadily all the way had turned into a full-blown storm. Wind was forcing twigs and leaves sideways, plastering them to my windshield. Earl ran over with an umbrella and told me, as he walked me to my door, that there was a girl at my door.

There was indeed a girl at my door, a small wet girl whom I realized, when I reached her, was a woman of about thirty. She was five feet tall at most, had long brown straight hair that the rain had plastered to her head. She was wrapped in an oversized trench coat tightly belted at the waist. When she saw me coming up the stairs, she reached into her pocket and handed me a piece of paper. I looked at it and then at her, wondering why she was showing me my own address.

"Vera Warsaly," she said, putting her hand out. "Simon from Sachs say you have room." Her voice, for such a small person, was surprisingly deep and rich.

"Oh yes!" I said. "Vera from Russia. Come in. I'll get towels and something warm to drink."

Simon worked with an organization that helped find homes for Russians fleeing the aftermath of the revolution. He had told me to expect Vera, but not for two weeks. He didn't know much about her background, beyond that she was, like so many other Russians after the revolution, a Bolshevik who was denounced as a traitor and sent to Siberia. She escaped by posing as the child of a government official who had been granted diplomatic leave. From the size of her, I could see that she would easily pass as a child, particularly if she didn't speak.

We stood in the hall and shook water out of our hair, grumbling and laughing about the downpour. I took her into the downstairs kitchen, ran up to my apartment for towels. After we were more or less dry and had enjoyed coffee and apple cake, I took her to the room I'd put aside for her on the main floor.

"Is all for me?" she asked, eyes wide in her tiny heart-shaped face. When I told her it was, she put her arms out and twirled. "So much room!" She patted the mattress and ran her hand along the green velvet wallpaper and laughed out loud when she opened the closet door and saw all the hangers. "This all I have," she said, pinching a piece of fabric on her dark gray skirt.

Two days later I came home to a transformed hallway. The floor was glowing; the red hall runner was free of dirt and lint and the big woven basket by the door, where my tenants dropped everything when they came in, was organized into separate piles of scarves, gloves, and hats. When I thanked Vera, she put one hand over her stomach and made a mock bow.

The main-floor kitchen was next. She got the rust stains out of the sink, moved the spices to a drawer beside the stove and arranged them, lying down, in alphabetical order. "Is more easy," she said.

I found her on her hands and knees in the downstairs bathroom a few days later with a pink and black kerchief tied over her hair, cleaning the grout between the floor tiles with a toothbrush.

"Vera," I said. "You don't have to do that. It's not important."

She stopped and sat back on her heels and looked up at me, each rubber glove big enough to hold three of her hands. "Is important for me," she said. "I like be busy." I felt badly for being so insensitive.

When Vera found a job at a Portuguese bakery two months later, she started paying rent but refused to stop cleaning.

"I have an idea," I said to her one day. We were in my upstairs kitchen dipping the Portuguese *biscoitos* she brought home regularly into hot, milky tea. The traffic below us was steady. Someone was hailing a taxi. "Why don't you help me with my Russian and I'll help you with your English?"

And so our lessons began. Monday evenings after dinner, sometimes late into the night, we drank English tea and spoke English.

Wednesday evenings we switched to vodka and Russian. We were both surprised at how much I remembered from my childhood lessons in Winnipeg.

* * *

Vera had grown up on a grain farm north of St. Petersburg in a hamlet called Tsvoet, which she said, like Podensk, was not on any map. She had two older brothers—Feodor and Herman—whom she adored.

Her parents sent her to St. Petersburg in her late teens to work for a rich family. They thought that being in service would be less stressful than life on the farm and hoped she would become a cook or a lady's maid.

"I think they hoping I find rich husband," she told me.

A few years before the revolution—she was head housekeeper by that point—she stopped to watch a Bolshevik rally in Manezhnaya Square. She'd had very little interest in politics until then.

"A man leap on statue. Is inside square. He talk about people rights and revolution and I believe everything he say."

Vera fell in love with Peter and joined the Bolshevik movement. She thought that justice would follow when the revolution was over, as he had told her it would. That there would be an end to the monarchy and the class system, more for the poor, less for the rich. But the Bolsheviks turned out to be no better than the tsars, maybe worse, she said. They took what they wanted and set up an organization of secret police called the Cheka to brutalize anyone who disapproved.

"Couldn't you go back to your parents' farm?" I asked.

Vera laughed. "Is no more farm, Anna. Is no more grain."

The Bolsheviks confiscated the grain to redistribute the seeds fairly, they claimed. Most of it rotted in warehouses, and what didn't was sold on the black market. Farmers were forced into the cities to line up for bread like everybody else.

For his part in the revolution, Peter was given a mansion abandoned by an aristocratic family in their rush to get out of the country. He expected Vera to move in with him.

She refused. One Sunday not longer after—she was walking down Divorg Boulevard—someone came up from behind her, pulled a pillowcase over her head, and took her to a prison in Moscow.

"Do you think Peter turned you in?"

"I not believe at first, but who else?"

"Did your family not know where you were? Do they now?"

"My family," Vera said, standing up, arching her back, and rubbing it. "Is enough talk. We go shopping. I need yellow sweater."

We walked through the streets of Chelsea arm in arm that day. It had been a warm winter. The sidewalks were clear and the sun strong.

"From now is only happy for me," she sighed and leaned into me. Her head ended at my shoulder.

"How come you not out with Cedric today?" Vera asked as we walked along. "Not flying?"

"I think Cedric and I are finished."

"Yes?"

"Yes. He's more interested in cocaine than he is in me."

"Is illegal now, no?"

"Yes. And he's filled the second bedroom in his apartment with Coca-Cola and Smitty's Cough Syrup so he doesn't run out. He wants me to get high with him. He says it makes you brighter, sharper, improves sex. Not for me. It makes me paranoid and my muscles twitch. He says I'm a prude. I don't seem to have much luck with relationships. The only man who ever accepted me for who I am was Nathaniel."

"Ah. Winnipeg boy. Where he is now?" she asked.

"I assume he's still in Winnipeg."

"He never contact you? You never contact him?"

"He wrote to me for a long time. He gave the letters to Esther and she sent them on to me. I never answered him. I didn't think he would ever forgive me for giving the baby up for adoption."

"Maybe he understand."

"No, Vera. He didn't forgive me. I saw him a few years ago on Thirty-Eighth Street when I was passing out Margaret's pamphlets."

"You never tell me this one," Vera said and stood waiting for an explanation.

* * *

It was around five in the afternoon. The street was crowded with shoppers and business people on their way home. I had passed out most of my pamphlets. A man wearing a big black hat had been standing across the street for some time with his hands in his coat pockets. He seemed to be watching me, which wasn't unusual. People would often stand just far enough away to glare at me and let me know they disapproved. A few days before a man had spat in my face, so when this one started walking toward me, I tensed.

"Hello Anna," he said.

Nobody else said my name that way and my heart leapt. He looked exactly as I had imagined he would when he was older—tall, narrow shoulders still, a little stooped. His beard was less red than I had expected, but fuller. His hair was still unruly, still reddish.

"Nathaniel," I said, resisting the impulse to throw my arms around him. "Is it really you?" I didn't know what to do with my pamphlets, with my face, with my racing heart.

"Anna," he said. His eyes were shining with delight. "You look the same."

Despite the more than twenty years that had passed, he looked the same too. "What are you doing in Manhattan?" I asked.

"I'm here on business and we have family here."

All I heard was the "we." It felt like someone had punched me in the stomach.

"How are your father and grandfather and grandmother Fayge?" I went on quickly. "She never liked me, I remember."

"Fayge died shortly after you left and my grandfather soon after that. Then my father a few years ago."

"I'm sorry to hear that. Do you have time for a coffee? There's a shop just around the corner. I'd love to talk with you."

We took a booth by the window. Nathaniel said it would be his treat.

"Good," I said. "Seeing you will be my treat."

"So," he said, smiling that wonderful, open smile. "Tell me everything."

I told him about the factories, the California Perfume Company, about my house, about how I had become an American citizen.

"What were you doing on that street corner?" he asked.

"Distributing birth control information."

He looked confused.

"Information on how to prevent pregnancies. I do volunteer work at birth control clinics as well."

"Isn't that illegal?"

"Yes. I've been arrested."

He shook his head. "You haven't changed, Anna. Except for your hair. What happened to your curls?"

Nathaniel had always loved my curls. He would run his fingers through them, try to make them spiral the other way.

I told him how, last year, I had made an appointment with my regular hairdresser, Antoine, to get a bob.

"A bob?"

"This," I said, lifting the right side of my hair with my palm. "A little shorter at the back and sleek. It's just becoming popular. Antoine tried to convince me that it was a mistake to cut my hair short. He showed me a newspaper article quoting a doctor who said that short haircuts cause migraines because of the exposure of the neck."

"How did you finally convince him?"

"I didn't. After he showed me the article, he went into his private room at the back of the salon. He stayed there for a full fifteen minutes—I timed it. Then his assistant came over and said that Antoine had fallen ill and would I please make another appointment. I went across the street to a barbershop. They knew just what I wanted and sold me a lifetime supply of Brylcreem to keep it smooth. I think Antoine didn't have the nerve to say no to me."

"No one ever did!" Nathaniel laughed and my heart ached with how much I loved that sound. It was like we had seen each other just last week.

When I finally got up the nerve to ask who "we" was, he told me about his wife, Mina, and their four children. It was an arranged marriage, he said. Mina was from Manhattan, but they lived in Winnipeg, in St. Boniface, where he was president of a company that designed and manufactured farm equipment.

"Do you remember St. Boniface?" he asked.

"Of course I do. We used to go to Provencher Park to feed the swans. Do you like it? Your work?"

"Yes, but I preferred designing to running the company."

"I remember that cutter you made to work with the plow in Moosomin, to get through the thick roots. Do you remember that?"

"I remember," he said. "I'm surprised you do."

"I haven't forgotten much," I said. "Do you remember the day I told you that I was leaving?"

"Yes," he said, a flicker of discomfort flashing across his face.

"I know it was a long time ago, but you said something that day that I can't forget. You said that you agreed with your grandmother that I was crazy like my mother. What did she mean? What did you mean?"

"That was a long time ago, Anna. I never thought you were crazy. I was just mad at you for going away."

"But why did your grandmother think my mother was crazy? Did she ever tell you?"

"She did."

"What did she say?"

He shook his head. "What does it matter now?"

"It does, Nathaniel. I've wanted to know for so long."

"Why?"

"I'd like to know, that's all."

He played with his coffee cup, took a deep breath, and our eyes met for long enough for me to feel myself flushing.

"You are incorrigible, you know."

"I know."

And he began. "My parents and your parents were close in Podensk. You knew that."

"Yes."

"Well, it goes back farther. Did you know that your mother had twin brothers?"

"No."

"Yes. When your mother was about seven—her brothers were thirteen or fourteen, I think—they were taken by the Russians for the army." He held up the finger with the tip his grandmother had cut off. "That's what this was all about. She was trying to save me from the Russian army.

"My grandmother says that your mother was there when her brothers were taken and it drove her crazy. That's why she sent you and Esther away. She was crazy with fear."

We sat quietly for a few moments. The bell on the door jingled and a man and a woman took the booth behind us, laughing as they sat down. I wanted so badly to reach out and touch him, to run my hand over his wounded finger.

"But why did Fayge think *I* was crazy?"

"Your wildness. Wearing boys' clothes. Leaving Winnipeg when you were so young. What does it matter now?"

He sounded resigned and took a sip of his coffee. "Did you ever marry, Anna?"

"No. Never found the right man. Maybe I'm afraid of getting too close."

"Don't you miss the intimacy? The emotional intimacy I mean, having someone who accepts you, the best and the worst and loves you in spite or maybe even because of it?"

"I think you were the only one who ever really accepted me, Nathaniel," I said and was sorry the moment the words left my mouth. "Now, enough of the past. Tell me why you're here."

"I'm not sure you want to know."

"I do."

He put down his coffee cup and put his elbows on the table, intertwined his fingers. He sighed.

"So many sighs, Nathaniel."

"I'm here to find our daughter."

The world stopped turning.

"How did you find out, Nathaniel?" I finally asked.

He smiled wearily. "Anna. Don't ask me that. It took years. I know you gave birth to her at the Evangeline Hospital on June 18, 1892. Don't you ever wonder what happened to her?"

* * *

I'm not sure when my desire to find out what had become of my child started. All I know is that as the years went by I found myself becoming mesmerized by a young mother wiping the ice cream off her daughter's face, or seeing a child sleeping on the El with his head knocking gently against his mother's shoulder. I realized I longed for that kind of connection.

In 1902, when my baby would have been ten, I made an appointment with the records clerk at the hospital where I had given birth. She was a tall middle-aged woman with a flat chest and a long face. I was sure she would tell me the records were closed, but she surprised me. She went right to a wall of filing cabinets, opened one of the drawers, and pulled out a folder. "I won't be able to tell you what happened to the baby," she said. "We don't record that kind of information, but I can tell you that she was recorded as Jane Doe, weighed eight pounds, three ounces, was twenty inches. Her BT, BP, HR, RR—all her vitals, that is—were normal."

She. I had had a girl.

I tried to read the signature on the bottom of the paper so I could find the doctor who'd delivered her, but couldn't decipher it. I did, however, see the initials DRWD printed under "Doctor" at the bottom of the page. I thanked the records clerk and went downstairs to the information desk where I found out that there was a doctor on staff with the initials DRWD—Dr. David Rutherford Wallace Drinkwater. I made an appointment to see him the next week.

He remembered the delivery. "This is a private hospital for end-of-life care," he said. "We don't do many deliveries, so I remember the few we do." The baby was normal, as far as he remembered, but he had no idea what had happened to her. "The nurse could have taken her home for all I know. If she was placed with an adoption agency, the records will be closed. There is one possibility, though a remote one. Hundreds of orphaned immigrant children are taken in by the New York Children's Aid Society every day. Some stay in the United States. They're adopted or put in orphanages. Some are put on what they call orphan trains and shipped to Mexico or Canada. There's a possibility that may have happened to her but I doubt it. Healthy newborns are in high demand."

I could have persevered. I could have found the nurse on duty that night. I could have hired a private detective. But then what? Would I stalk her? Introduce myself? Write to her parents and ask if I could see her? I gave it up as a lost cause.

* * *

"You had no right to go away without telling me that you were pregnant, Anna," Nathaniel said to me that day in the restaurant. "No right to give her away. She's my child too. It's exactly what my grandmother says your mother did with you and Esther. She sent you away without even discussing it with your father. Only I'm going to find her."

• CHAPTER TWENTY-ONE •

If I had been a few minutes late for my volunteer shift at the new Myrtle Street birth control clinic in Brooklyn that frigid Friday morning in December, my life might have played out differently. Perhaps Esther's would have too. I could have been there for her when Charles died and then the Count. I might have prevented the catastrophe that followed.

But I wasn't late. I was early. Even though it was my first day at this clinic, I was hoping to get away before four to drive to the sanatorium. Esther had called the night before to say that Charles had had another relapse and I promised her that I would try to get there Friday night instead of Saturday morning.

Myrtle Street Medical was the fifth birth control clinic I'd volunteered at since I'd begun working with Margaret Sanger three years earlier. The other four had been closed down by the police within weeks of their opening. This time Margaret had hired a lawyer and taken his advice. On paper, Myrtle Street would operate as a clinic for preventing venereal disease, which was legal.

My job was always the same. I helped the women fill out the necessary forms, prepared them for the fact that a doctor was going to do an internal examination, and then explained their birth control options. My conversational Russian helped, as many of our clients were Eastern European immigrants.

I wasn't surprised anymore at the bizarre birth control methods these women had been using: wearing the bones of black cats around their necks; rubbing the spit of a virgin on their bellies before having sex; drinking a mixture of oil and quicksilver after.

* * *

I first heard Margaret speak in front of the Sloane Maternity Hospital in June of 1915. I didn't know her at the time, but knew of her. She was in the news so often it was almost impossible not to. She opened new birth control clinics as quickly as the authorities closed the existing ones down. She also published and distributed a newspaper called *The Woman Rebel*. And it was she who coined the term "birth control."

About twenty women were gathered to hear her that day at the hospital. Her taxi pulled up just before two and we all watched her step out, a briefcase in one hand and a small stepstool in the other. Even though I had seen pictures of her in the paper, I was surprised at how conventionally pretty she was with a gray silk scarf tied fashionably around her forehead. I had expected her to be more forbidding looking somehow. She paid the taxi driver and then turned and smiled at us.

She put her stool down and stepped up on it. Several nurses came out of the hospital, closed the gate behind them, and joined us on the sidewalk.

"Thank you for coming here today, ladies," she said. "I can see all the negative publicity about me is working." We laughed. "Being gagged and jailed silences me momentarily but it makes so many more of you aware of my cause." She looked at her watch quickly and then back at us. "I suspect the hospital will call the police once they know I'm here, so our time is limited.

"Most of you know that I'm a nurse by profession, but I am also a daughter and a mother, though not very good at managing all three." We laughed again. "I haven't practiced nursing for over nineteen years. I stopped the day my mother died. She'd had eighteen pregnancies in twenty-two years and died of tuberculosis and cervical cancer. I promised myself at her deathbed that I would not take another nursing case until all working women in America had legal access to birth control."

Gesturing to the hospital behind her, she said, "There are physicians inside this very hospital who help middle- and upper-class women like you prevent pregnancies and terminate them. It's time that civility—that right—was passed along to the women who need it most."

We heard the sirens then. Most of the women took off. The three of us who stayed, along with Mrs. Sanger, were put into the back of a police van and taken to the City Prison. I shivered when I saw where we were, afraid that it was going to be a repeat of the experience I'd had earlier, the weekend I found out that Jack was married.

It wasn't. We were escorted to a large, bright room on the main floor that looked more like a meeting room than a prison cell. It was carpeted in a flat brown and black weave. A soft green sofa sat along one wall, two matching armchairs across from it with a large coffee table between them. I commented to no one in particular that I was surprised we weren't being served coffee. A few moments later, a woman in a gray uniform wheeled in a trolley with a carafe of coffee, a carafe of cold water, cups, cream and sugar, and biscuits. Everyone laughed.

Mrs. Sanger, who was on the sofa beside me, undid the top button of her jacket and invited us all to get comfortable. "We're going to be here until my lawyer arrives so we might as well relax." She reached her hand out to me. "Nice to meet you. I'm Margaret Sanger."

I laughed at her humility. "I know who you are," I said. "My name is Anna Grieve."

"Are you with the movement?"

"Not formally," I said. "I work for the California Perfume Company."

The look on her face told me exactly what she thought of women who sold bath salts door-to-door for a living.

"Wait," I said. "I've been selling womb veils to my customers for years."

Interested again, she sat forward. "How do you manage that?"

I told her what I did and how I did it. I talked about my womb veil trick and the women chuckled sympathetically.

"That's brilliant," she said. "How did you become interested in birth control?"

"Two friends had unwanted pregnancies. One had an abortion. The other gave her child up for adoption. Both were heartbreaking."

"Yes," she said, stirring the sugar into her cup thoughtfully. "Most of us got involved through personal experience."

We talked for hours in that room, sharing stories and fantasizing about what the world could be like. When they let us out, I could see that Margaret's celebrity was working for her. The matron who escorted us to the door actually told her it was good to see her again.

* * *

Three years later, a confirmed Sanger supporter by then, I was walking up the stairs of the new Myrtle Street Clinic hoping to get away early to see Esther and Charles at the sanatorium. Two weeks of November drizzle followed by minus six temperatures had turned the city into a skating rink. Although I was wearing boots with a deep tread, the stairs were still treacherous. I remember thinking I'd have to get someone to clean them before the clients started arriving.

The last thing I remember about that morning is reaching for the doorknob and the door flying open in my face. I regained consciousness in a small windowless room with a group of people I had never seen before. I found out much later that we were in the same prison where I had met Margaret, and the people I was with were the staff of the new clinic. Over the course of the day, they all left. They'd been born in the United States and had the good sense to say so.

I had no sense at all. My head was aching, my vision was fuzzy, I couldn't stand up without falling over, and I was nauseated. I had no idea who I was or where I was. I felt like a two-year-old child waiting for someone to come and take me back to where I should be. I had no identification with me, I remembered much later, because I hadn't been able to find my wallet that morning and had grabbed a change purse and some tissues and put them into my coat pocket.

Several times during the course of the next few days, the police questioned me.

"What is your name, Miss?"

I didn't know.

"Where do you live, Miss?"

I didn't know.

"Do you have a job? Is there anyone you'd like to call? Where were you born?"

That one I knew. "Russia."

The deportation of "Reds" was just starting in the United States at that point. Americans were afraid, with everything that was going on in the world, that anarchy and communism were on the rise and were blaming everything from strikes to race riots on eastern European anarchists. The president had even approved a sedition act and an espionage act to make getting rid of undesirable aliens easier.

I was transferred to Ellis Island on the second day, given a cursory deportation hearing, convicted of breaching the Sedition Act, and escorted onto the Finnish freighter *Nymphe* to be taken "back" to St. Petersburg.

My cabin was a six-by-eight room below deck next to the engine room. It felt like it was ninety-eight degrees at all times and the sound of coal being shoveled never stopped. I came to love that sound. I would sit in my room and count the number of shovel scrapes—one, two, three, four, five, and then it would stop. I would hold my breath and count again—one, two, three, four, five, and *bam!* The coal would hit the inside of the furnace and tumble down.

My spells of panic were few and far between because until I remembered who I was, nothing seemed abnormal. Memories came back slowly, in fragments: my mother feeding me with a spoon; walking with Esther on the grounds of the sanatorium; Vera's face.

Every four hours, my coal-shoveling firemen would gather outside my door to change shifts. They would laugh and roughhouse. I finally got up the nerve to open my door when they were there one day, and they went silent. One of them tucked his shirt into his pants and bowed and put his hand out to shake mine. His buddy elbowed him in the ribs, said something in Russian, and showed him how to do it; he spit on his hand, wiped it on his pants, and *then* put it out for a shake.

I started to join them for meals and was pleased that I had enough Russian to have simple conversations. They were a good lot. They taught me a card game, the words to a lewd Russian song, how to fart on demand. I often opened my door in the morning to a small gift—a piece of dark chocolate wrapped in brown paper, writing paper and a dull pencil, a down pillow to replace the woolen blanket that had been rubbing my cheeks raw.

Only one of the firemen ever made a pass at me. He knocked on my door late one night, and when I opened it, threw his cap on my cot and gave me his best toothless grin. He was polite when I gave him his cap back and shook my head.

I knew, by that point, who I was and that we were on our way to St. Petersburg, where I was sure I would be able to sort things out.

After twenty-eight days on the *Nymphe*, two skinny young men in black, tightly belted leather coats walked me off the ship and onto a wharf. It was so quiet, I thought I had gone deaf. When one of the sailors yelled down at me, "Anna, Anna," I realized that I wasn't deaf. It was just that the sound of the shoveling was gone.

It was dark on the wharf, the only light coming from the moon, a few stars, and the glowing tips of the cigarettes in the mouths of a few sailors on deck. The skinny young men walked me to a long, black car with a uniformed driver in the front. The three of us got in the backseat with me sandwiched in the middle. We drove for hours, the driver moving his head back and forth as if he was hearing music. Nobody spoke.

As the sun came up, we passed a railway station with tall black light standards that followed the tracks as far as I could see and turned onto a winding narrow street where feral dogs were looking for food and women in housecoats were leaning in their doorways, watching us. The city got brighter, the streets wider, the buildings more sophisticated. We stopped at last in front of a beautiful old mansion. The driver came around and opened the back door and we got out. It was bitterly cold and bitingly clear.

"Anna Grieve," a man walking toward me said. He put a fur coat over my shoulders and held out a gloved hand. "My name is Mason

Tate. I'm the American attaché stationed here. I'll help you sort everything out."

"What day is it?" I asked, the bright light making my eyes tear. "Where am I?"

"It's December second," he said. "And you're in St. Petersburg."

"What year is it?"

"Nineteen eighteen."

"Am I under arrest?"

"No, Ma'am, you are not. We apologize for the trouble. You're free to go back to the United States. But first we have to make sure you have the right documentation and we have to get you to a doctor. I've been told that you have a head injury. Is that correct?"

I was relieved. Margaret must have figured out what had happened and sorted things out. I thought then that it would be a matter of days until I went home. It turned out to be seven months. I didn't know it at the time, but the Americans had refused to acknowledge the post-revolutionary Bolshevik government and were closing the Embassy in St. Petersburg. My travel papers were the last thing on anyone's mind.

"I have to call my sister," I said to Mr. Tate.

"She's been notified," he told me. "Let's get you to your hotel. You must be freezing."

February 12, 1919
Dear Esther,
Today I got two of your letters, one written fourteen days ago and one written two months ago. I believe now that all the mail is being filtered through the Central Committee. You may have written more and you may not be getting everything I've sent you. So forgive me if I don't answer your questions in the order that you've asked them. Mason Tate from the American Embassy says he puts my letters in with the

diplomatic pouches and that yours come the same way. But I don't think anything here is immune to Soviet snooping.

You ask what it's like to be staying in the Grand Konstantin Hotel. Compared to what the Count and Countess have told us about the place, it's not recognizable. Remember how they talked about the central marble staircase? The mirrored wall tiles filigreed with gold in the lobby and the rock crystal chandelier? The stairs are still there but everything else is gone. The chandelier, the mirrored tiles. Everything that can be lifted has been sold on the black market.

My room is large. I wish it were smaller because it might be warmer. There's a small furnace in the basement, but it rarely works and when it does, it doesn't bring the heat up to the third floor. I doubt that it ever did. There's a fireplace in my room, but nothing to burn. I sleep on a large bed with a thin, lumpy mattress. I have three thin gray wool blankets, each too short to cover my body. When I lie down, I arrange one over my feet, one under my chin and the third over the space in between. I tried using the fur coat that Mason gave me as a blanket, but the fur got in my nose and made me sneeze all night. So I use the blankets and if I don't move, I stay covered. There's a small sink in the room with cold running water. It doesn't run really. It drips. But I'm lucky compared to what I see on the streets. The people look more like rats than human beings, scurrying along in rags, bent over, pouncing on anything that could be eaten or sold.

Mason Tate often sends over the remains of Embassy functions—cheeses and fancy French desserts and I gobble them down with my hands, thinking of how upset the Countess would be to see me eating that way. Yesterday one of his minions brought me caviar and little toast points. Other than that, I eat in the hotel dining room with the revolutionaries living here; gray soup with unrecognizable things floating in it and hunks of stale bread.

I'm still wearing the clothes I arrived in, except for my underwear. I have only one pair now, Russian, that somebody from the Embassy found for me; big and gray and itchy. My good underwear was stolen when I went down to the basement to wash it in the huge copper tubs down there. I hung the panties on the ropes near the furnace to dry and they were gone the next morning. I have only the itchy wool ones left and I don't want to lose them, so I wash them in my room every night and hang them over the sink to dry. I go to bed hoping that they'll be dry by morning. It's horrible when they're not. I did try to get my stolen underpants replaced, but you have to fill out three different official requests and take them to three different offices where they stamp the form, put it on top of a pile of other forms and tell you they will get in touch with you if the items are returned.

I don't know when I'll be coming home, Esther. I see the Embassy doctor every two weeks. He says it's a brain injury and the effects could be long lasting, but not to worry, he says I'm coming along well although it could be months before I'm well enough to travel. I suspect it may take that long to get my documentation straightened out as well. Things don't move very quickly here.

Let me say again how sorry I am that I wasn't there for you when Charles died and then the Count. I was shocked to hear about him. I didn't even know he was ill. It does sound like you're coping admirably though. Probably better than I am at this point.

Your loving sister Bencke

P.S. Two P.S.s actually.
Thank you for contacting Vera and offering to help with house expenses. I haven't received a letter from her yet, but I know she'll appreciate it and it's a load off my mind.

I'm concerned that you're thinking about closing your house and taking an apartment in St. Boniface. I know the house is too big for you now but they say you shouldn't make any major decisions for a year after the loss of a loved one. You've lost two, Esther, and you don't even know how to boil water!

The Count's death didn't hit me until months later. When I first read about it in Esther's letter, I was more concerned about how it would affect her. But if she was telling me the truth, she seemed to have everything under control.

* * *

Certainly nothing was under control for me. I didn't know anyone other than Mason Tate and he was away from the Embassy more often than he was there. The Embassy itself was disturbing. Every time I went there, more furniture was gone: the filing cabinets were gone on one visit; a credenza on the next. I never saw the same person twice, and whoever was at the front desk always seemed distracted. They opened a drawer, looked for my file, closed the drawer, said my travel documents would be ready before the Embassy closed. They confirmed that they had contacted Vera and I would just have to wait for her letters. The few times they let me use the phone, all I got was static.

It was like suddenly being nobody. I had no money, no home, no papers, no friends. I could have died on the street and no one would have known.

My suit hung on me. I could see my hipbones and feel my cheekbones. My sleek bob was a mass of curls again. I knew that in Manhattan, with a little kohl around my eyes and the right clothes, I would look like a model, but here I looked like everyone else, hungry and afraid, which I was.

I started to find coincidences and meaningless events providential: if I wake up and the blankets haven't shifted, then Mason will get my papers today; if the old man I saw on the street yesterday is there again, I'll get a letter from Vera.

I started to think that people were following me; that something terrible was going to happen. Nights, I stayed in my freezing hotel room, wrapped in my fur, reading and rereading a copy of *War and Peace* that Mason Tate had given me. It felt so odd to be sitting in a once-grand Russian hotel reading about the days when this very hotel was the center of aristocratic life.

Days, I walked the devastated city, overwhelmed by the brutality and loss. I saw elegant apartment buildings, three- and four-story baroque structures with wrought-iron balconies and large central courtyards, rats as huge as cats scurrying through them. I saw old women and young children and soldiers in tattered greatcoats, standing in long lines waiting for their daily ration of three-quarters of a loaf of bread. I watched squatters hanging political banners in the windows of abandoned mansions, rough-looking men butting their cigarettes in gardens that still had vestiges of order and beauty. I saw people ripping boards from the windows of the once-fine shops along Nevsky Prospect. It was still a broad and handsome street, but stripped now of all promise.

If Mamma and Pappa were still alive, what had the revolution done to them, I wondered. It sickened me to think that they had suffered in their old age while Esther and I had lived in such comfort.

One afternoon in March—I had been in St. Petersburg for almost four months—I decided to stop worrying about myself and do something for someone else. I had read a section in *War and Peace* the night before that had inspired me.

Here I am alive, I had read . . . *it's not my fault, so I have to try and get by as best I can without hurting anybody.*

I took two hard-boiled eggs that the Embassy had sent over the day before, wrapped them in a kerchief, and walked to the Griboedov Canal to find a young woman I had seen prostituting herself there several times. I felt the warmth of the sun for the first time since my arrival as I left the hotel. It felt like my bones were thawing. The young woman was there, blond, skeletal, wearing the same long gray wool dress with several matted and shrunken wool sweaters over it.

"Please take this," I said, holding out the kerchief with the eggs.

She looked me over, stepped forward, and took the kerchief from my hand. She opened it, saw the eggs, and then looked me over again more slowly. Her lips were raw and chafed, red all the way up to her nose. She had light blue eyes, blond eyelashes and eyebrows.

"*Ty khocheshmenyayebat?*" she asked. "You want fuck me?" The look on her face was contemptuous.

I shook my head and told her in Russian that I wanted nothing.

She looked down at the eggs again, at my fur coat, which I realize must have seemed like a luxury to her, then folded the corners of the kerchief back over the eggs, put the kerchief in a pocket of her dress, moved closer to me, and spat in my face.

"Don't be upset," a male voice behind me said.

I turned to see a tall man with a long black coat draped over his shoulders and a printed navy silk scarf tied around his neck. He was broad and barrel-chested with a square, clean-shaven face and deep-set pale gray eyes like a wolf's. So tall that my head ended at his shoulders.

"I've seen you walking here before," he said. "You're American."

"No, yes," I said. "It's complicated."

"My name is Oscar Arkhangelsk," he said, holding out a brown leather-gloved hand. "I see that you're disturbed by what just happened.

Let me take you for tea. I can help you understand why things are in such a sorry state at the moment."

"No thank you," I said. My response to him had been instant, strong, and sexual.

Over the next week, I saw him on the canal three more times. Each time he stopped and said hello, his coat always around his shoulders, his manner slightly reserved, amused, as if he knew it was just a matter of when. The third time, I agreed to go for tea. I'd been thinking about him and hoped if I spent some time with him, I would find him less appealing. I didn't want any complications in my life. I wanted my concussion to clear, my papers to arrive, and my time in St. Petersburg to be over.

As we walked, he put his hand on my back to turn corners, under my elbow to help me over uneven pavement. I hoped he couldn't sense how I was responding to his touch. He smiled whenever our eyes met, a slow smile, his lips together.

"You don't have to be afraid," he said when he stopped in front of a dilapidated brick building with garbage and broken glass on the grounds. "There's a coffee house around the back."

He guided me down a short flight of stairs to a shiny black door. I was nervous about going in but the smell of coffee and yeast and sugar was irresistible. He knocked. A male voice answered tersely in Russian. He replied as tersely and the door was opened from inside. We stepped down three stairs into a large, square room with low ceilings.

Everything in the room was white except for the floor, which was shiny black concrete. About a dozen small round tables were spaced around the room, a short white starched cloth over each, a shiny silver samovar in the center. Most of the tables were occupied, three or four people around them, mostly men in Cheka uniforms. There were a few women, beautifully dressed. I felt self-conscious in my ratty, oversized fur.

Several of the people looked up at Oscar as we passed them, obviously prepared to say hello but he ignored them. I should have known then that something was not right. He guided me to an empty table at the back, beside a glassed-in pastry station that was filled with cakes and croissants and tiered tortes and cheese cakes and a dessert I thought I'd never see again called the King's Cake.

I was dizzy with desire. Mamma used to make King's Cake for us. Esther and I would stand at her side waiting impatiently until she had given the batter the exact number of strokes. "Out of my way, little foxes," she would say. "Watching won't make it go faster." Finally, she would pour the cake into a baking pan, scraping out as much of the batter as she could, Esther and I delirious by then to lick out the bowl. She used six eggs, I remember, and sour cream and cocoa powder and poppy seeds and walnuts and a secret ingredient she told us she had added on her own, three teaspoons of vinegar, to make it rise. The icing was creamed butter and sugar.

Oscar took his coat off and folded it over the back of his chair. He sat smiling at me, waiting for something. When I saw that the left arm of his jacket was pinned to his lapel and his arm was missing, he relaxed and gestured to the pastry station. "Would you like something?"

I declined.

"They're very good. Made right here," he said.

"How can this be?" I asked, the saliva so thick in my mouth I had trouble speaking. "The people outside are starving."

"The people outside as you call them," he said with an almost cruel smile, "won't always be starving. Things are changing for the better."

"Forgive me," I said. My hunger was making me lightheaded and fearless. "I've just arrived. I don't know you and I don't know anything about Russian politics and I barely speak the language. But I don't see things changing for the better."

"You're right," he said, the smile never leaving his face. "You *weren't* here before the revolution so you don't have a comparison. A revolution is a process. It isn't simply taking from the rich and giving to the poor. The people outside, as you call them, wouldn't know what to do with power or with money. It would be madness, handing everything over to them, like turning a jail over to the inmates, or an asylum to the lunatics. These things are organic and take time. It's admirable that you feel so strongly. We all do. That was the point. That *is* the point."

I ended up having two pieces of King's Cake and a cup of coffee that was so good I moaned with the first sip.

Over the next few months Oscar took me to see what he called the future of Russia.

He took me to a fashion design house in a private mansion now owned by the Bolsheviks, where men and women in gray smocks were working side-by-side designing and sewing what Oscar called the clothes of the future—minimalist uniform-like suits in stiff canvas and coarse calico and wool, grays and blacks, the only adornment geometric patterned black and gray scarves that reminded me of the Cubist art that was so popular at the time.

We went to a high school where teenagers with bright eyes and clean hair were gathered in small groups, poring over maps and engine parts and animal skeletons. He took me to the Winter Palace, where we watched attendants wearing white gloves wrap and label what was left of the Romanov linen, china, and silver. "Future generations will come here and see the obscene waste of the monarchy," he said. "One day the whole world will understand."

We went to political meetings where dozens of men and women, most of them as well-dressed as Oscar, spoke passionately about the future and thrust their clenched fists in the air. Oscar often spoke at these meetings. It was obvious that he was respected and admired. It stirred me, all this passion and purpose. It reminded me of the street corner speeches I had heard in Manhattan.

"But what about the famine in the Urals?" I asked him on the way home from one meeting. I had been to the Embassy earlier that day and seen an American newspaper saying that Russia was sinking under the yoke of Communism. "What about the farmers being so hungry that they're eating their seeds instead of planting them? How can you all talk about the future with all this devastation going on in the country?"

"It's propaganda, Anna," he said. "Surely coming from America you know about propaganda. I thought you were sophisticated enough not to believe everything you hear or read. Don't you know what's happening in America now? People like Emma Goldman are there, working for our cause."

I wondered if Oscar was right. If the American government had deported me because they thought I was a threat to democracy, what else were they willfully misrepresenting?

"Give it time," he said and I did. I even started helping him translate the political pamphlets he was smuggling into the United States into colloquial English.

Oscar fed me and clothed me, brought me tortoiseshell combs for my hair and silk underwear to replace the pair I had lost. I would wake up some mornings wondering where he was only to have him return shortly with coffee in an earthenware pitcher and buns. He brought a whole King's Cake one morning and we ate far too much of it before we fell back into bed.

When I told him one day how much I loved the architecture of the old Mariinsky Theatre, he bought tickets. We saw a play called *A New*

Beginning, written by a Russian playwright, whose only claim to fame, as far as I could see, was his membership in the party. It was a heavy-handed piece about the absence of beauty in bourgeois life. I found it bourgeois and lacking in beauty itself, but Oscar told me I had missed the subtleties and it did get a standing ovation.

One afternoon in May, we walked by a grove of lilacs just starting to bud, tiny purple nubs filling the air. It took me back to the Count's lilac trees in Winnipeg. He had his lilacs imported from Russia and was so devoted to them that he wouldn't let the gardeners touch them. He dug alkaline compost around the roots every spring, deadheaded the blossoms exactly one month after they had bloomed. I used to sit under the heavy branches when he worked in the grove, inhaling the heady scent.

I don't know who was more shocked when I started to cry, Oscar or me. He took me back to the hotel, took my shoes off and rubbed my feet and lay down beside me and dried my tears while I told him about the Count, about how much I missed him.

"If it weren't for him I wouldn't be who I am today. I wouldn't be nearly as sympathetic to your cause," I wept, "and I'll never be able to tell him now how much he meant to me."

Oscar listened and stroked my forehead and kissed my face. We fell asleep fully clothed in each other's arms.

Sitting cross-legged on the bed in my room one evening, I told him a little bit about Vera. I was reluctant to give him her name or tell him where she lived. After all, the Bolsheviks had sent her to Siberia and despite all his passion and high principles, Oscar was still a Bolshevik.

"I have a friend, Oscar," I said. "She came to the United States from Siberia a few years ago. She was a Bolshevik until the revolution. She became a Menshevik after."

Oscar chuckled. "Mensheviks."

"Don't dismiss me, Oscar. She was sent to Schlusselburg, you know it?"

"Of course I know it," he said. "It hasn't been used since the dark ages."

That's not what Vera had told me. She told me that Schlusselburg had been built as a medieval fortress on the Neva River and been turned into a prison for people like her after the revolution. The cells were sacks, she said. They opened at the top to drop in prisoners and food and water. She lived in her own feces for three weeks. When they saw she was pregnant, they sent her to a work camp in Siberia. She had her baby there, a little boy, and either he froze to death or she killed him so he wouldn't freeze. She never told me which.

"Anna," Oscar said, "that's a terrible story. And it's not the only one. Your friend sounds like she suffered greatly and I am sorry. But you mustn't abandon the cause for its mistakes."

I started to wonder whether Vera had exaggerated the situation or whether Oscar was lying to me. There were enough things about our relationship that didn't seem right.

Sometimes I confronted him. Why did we spend all our time at my hotel room rather than where he lived? Why had I never met his family or friends? Why did he never introduce me to people at the coffee house or at the meetings? We always arrived at meetings after they had started and he whisked me out possessively the moment they were over.

I thought at first that maybe it was because I was so badly dressed, but even after I started wearing the clothes Oscar brought me, that didn't change and he always had a reasonable answer. I never met his family because he was an only child and his parents were dead. Most of his friends had been killed in the war. He would be embarrassed to take me to his room in the "hovel" he said he shared with ten other men. And the pièce de résistance—he would introduce me to people in the party when he knew I was committed to him and the cause.

* * *

I shifted the car into third.

"Oscar, I hope this is worth it," I said. "It's been over thirty years. It would be a miracle if Podensk is still there."

"Well," Oscar said, "miracles happen. We met."

"I'm not sure that can be categorized as a miracle. I thought at first you were stalking me."

"I suppose I was in a way. I was so moved by your giving food to that wretched little creature, I had to meet you."

I was having trouble with the gear box.

"Sorry I can't help you with the driving. We can stop whenever you like."

I glanced at him. He was so big, so tall, his knees crunched at his chest in the passenger seat. "When I get tired, we can stop. In the meantime, I'm enjoying driving again, even this old thing. However did you get an American car?"

"Someone owed me a favor."

The gear engaged finally.

"Oscar," I said as we moved forward, "tell me what happened."

"How what happened?"

"You know what I'm talking about."

"What good would it do?"

"I would get to know you better. That's good enough."

He sighed and looked out the window. "Now is as good a time as any, I guess. It was nineteen fifteen," he said, reliving it. "I was with the

Russian Third Army in Poland. The Germans had just been defeated in France. We were in the foothills of the Carpathian Mountains. They're so beautiful, Anna. We'll go through areas like that. I'll point them out—waterfalls and mineral springs and mountain ranges so steep you can't see their tops.

"Left here," he shouted suddenly and I turned onto a steep, barely cleared road with scraggly shrubs and trees on either side. The path was so foreshortened, I couldn't see more than five feet in front of me, and the incline was getting steeper. "I don't want to tell you the rest," he said, his reverie shattered. "There was an explosion, flesh hanging from trees. If I say any more I won't get it out of my head."

Even now, after everything that happened, I feel a stirring in my chest when I think of Oscar's passionate outbursts; how he would pace around my room like a caged bear, gesturing to make a point, hitting his chest with a fist, running his hand through his thick, wavy brown hair.

"Short skirts and knee rouge and dancing on tables in Harlem?" he would say about my life in America. "Flying lessons, movie houses, and contraband gin? At least here you can get vodka legally." He would always end his diatribes with a plea that I stay in St. Petersburg with him. "We'll be like Emma Goldman and Alexander Berkman. We'll overthrow the yoke of imperialism and live meaningful lives."

* * *

Rather than taking the short inland route from St. Petersburg to Podensk, Oscar had planned a route that would let me see what he called the real Russia.

"That," he said as we passed a sprawling yellow brick mansion set back on a huge estate, "was the summer home of the tsar's right hand-man, Count Galizen-Shuyskies."

"Where is he now?" I asked, almost afraid to hear the answer.

"This particular family escaped to Paris before the revolution. They knew what was coming." He laughed, a harsh bark. "His wife, the countess, is making hats for Chanel, and he's driving a cab. They're lucky. The vermin that didn't get away and are still alive are digging graves or cleaning toilets in public buildings."

Late that afternoon we arrived at a farm where Oscar had arranged for us to spend the night. Owned by friends of his who were in St. Petersburg for the weekend, the picture-postcard white frame farmhouse had a wrap-around porch, and hundred-foot larches shading the house and dappling the grounds. A shiny black mare with a glistening foal at her rump stood watching us from a picket fenced paddock, tails twitching.

"This is what it will all be like soon, Anna. You'll see."

He asked me in bed that night if I was happy.

"I'm happy with you, Oscar, but I'm still disturbed by the contradictions I see."

He threw the covers off and sat up, his eyes flat and cold. "Why do you keep harping on the same things? I'm making your stay in St. Petersburg comfortable. Don't be naïve. It doesn't suit you."

• CHAPTER TWENTY-TWO •

M r. McGirk slides a colored map of the cemetery across his desk to me.

He's a natty little man with thin lips and glossy fingernails. The nameplate on his desk reads *Mr. M.W. McGirk, Funeral Director.*

"Your sister's husband chose this spot," he says, guiding a slender wooden pointer across the map. "As you can see, it's right beside his resting place on this slight hillock in the west compound. The plots in this compound are larger, four feet of planting space rather than the two elsewhere in the cemetery."

He gives me a conspiratorial isn't-it-wonderful-that-we-don't-have-to-worry-about-money-at-a-time-like-this smile. "There's ample space for drains and water pipes and the vista—well, the vista speaks for itself. It's wonderful." His pointer sweeps along a curving path. "This area can be tended regularly, of course, for an additional fee if family members are not available."

"I understand."

"There's another choice as well," and he moves his pointer a little to the west. "Mr. Kinnear thought Mrs. Kinnear might like to be closer to Count and Countess Chernovski for her final resting place. This

plot is equidistant from his and her parents'. Did she make her prefer-
ence clear to you, or is it in her will?"

"Is there any way I can see the actual cemetery before I make a
decision?" I ask.

"Of course you can, Miss Grieve. There's a gatekeeper on duty
twenty-four hours, seven days a week. He has a cart to take patrons
over the grounds if they don't want to walk. The roads are quite pass-
able though, even in this weather. We keep them cleared. I'll give you
this map to take with you."

I walk to the cemetery the next morning. It's overcast, the sky
almost white against the gigantic evergreens. The gatekeeper offers to
drive me to the plot in his little open vehicle but I tell him I'd prefer
to walk. Gentle hills and stands of bare birches are dotted among the
towering evergreens. The headstones are tasteful, granite and bronze
mostly, in grays and pinks and black-browns. There are a few mausole-
ums faced with marble. The map Mr. McGirk has given me is good. I
find the site with no problem.

So different from what Oscar and I found in Podensk.

* * *

Oscar and I weren't speaking when we left the farm where we had spent
the night. I was upset about his lashing out at me and we were quiet
for several hours.

"Please stop," Oscar said at about noon. "We need to talk."

We were on a dirt road that curved along the Volga, as flat and
reflective as a mirror.

"Anna, don't be upset with me," he said, leaning over to kiss my
cheek. "Let's stop and have some lunch." His friends at the farm had
left us a basket lunch. "Tell me what I did wrong."

"It felt like you were threatening me last night, Oscar. You told me I was naïve, that you were making St. Petersburg comfortable for me. What's the alternative? Turning me over to the Cheka?"

"How can you even think that? I would never hurt you. You're everything to me. Please forgive me. I know I have a bad temper. I'll be more thoughtful, I promise."

* * *

I was ready to leave the moment we arrived. It was nothing but charred stumps and rubble. I wasn't even sure we were in the right place.

"If this is Podensk," I said, getting out of the car, "we should be able to see the turrets of Chernovski Castle to the east. Let's forget this, Oscar. It was a bad idea in the first place."

Oscar insisted that we walk to a little cemetery a short distance away. "You might recognize some of the names," he said.

"It could be any cemetery, Oscar. There are so many of them and they all look the same around here. Please, let's just consider it a bad idea and go back to St. Petersburg."

"We've come this far," he insisted. "Let's walk through."

I didn't want to have another argument, so I agreed. It was a hot June day and the earth was parched-looking. Oscar took my hand. I didn't want the physical contact but pulling my hand away would only have increased the tension between us, so I acquiesced.

An old woman kneeling at a grave lifted her head and watched us weave around the markers, most of them stone, lying flat over the graves. A few were upright, wooden, leaning more than standing, cut into various shapes with names burned or carved into them. It was starting to feel familiar.

We passed one—taller than the others with intersecting lines carved down the sides and two names between them. A small shock went through me as I realized we were in the right place. I remembered Mamma telling Esther and me it was the grave of the old rabbi and his wife. She pulled me away once when I started to dance around it and told me that was forbidden.

"Do any of the names look familiar?" Oscar asked.

"Maybe," I said, running my hand over another marker so weathered and dry a large shard of wood came off in my hand as I touched it. I looked at the marker more closely.

Leo Grieve—born 1840, died 1883, devoted husband of Anit, loving father of Esther and Anna.

Dropping the shard as if my hand had been burned, I turned to Oscar and said, "It's him. It's my father." I was having trouble breathing.

Oscar picked up the piece of wood I had dropped and put it in his pocket. "Come." He held his hand out for me. "Let's see if we can find your mother's grave."

"Maybe it was destroyed," I said as we walked through the graveyard. "Mamma's would be beside Pappa's."

"What was her full name?" Leo asked.

"Anit Grieve," I said, the name catching in my throat. "Anit Dvora Grieve. She was born in eighteen forty-four I think." And with no warning, my knees buckled and I fell to the ground.

When I had stopped crying, Oscar helped me up. He gave me his handkerchief and told me to wait while he went to the car. He came back with a roll of heavy white paper and a piece of charcoal. "I'll hold the paper in place and you rub the charcoal over it," he said, walking to my father's grave. "It will give you something to remember him by and Esther will want to see this, I'm sure."

"Excuse me." It was the old woman we had seen kneeling. Her face was papery with cross-hatched lines, and a heavy brown kerchief was pulled almost to her eyebrows. "This is a Jewish cemetery," she said. "You can't do that." She put her hand on my father's marker. "He was a good man, Leo."

My heart was racing. I asked her if she knew him well.

"Yes, of course. Who are you?"

"I'm Anna," I said. "Anna Grieve."

"Are you?" she asked suspiciously, coming closer and staring up at me with milky white eyes. "You just might be," she said slowly. "I'm Sophie Feinhut, Baruch's sister. You remember Baruch?"

"Maybe, Mrs. Feinhut. Do you know what happened to my mother? I can't find her grave."

"Your mother's not here. She went away after your father died, after his accident. Do you remember the accident?"

"Yes," I said. "I think I do. The men brought him home lying on a door." She reached up and touched my cheek and a shock went through me. "Little Bencke Grieve," she said. "You just might be. You look like your mother a little bit. Her eyes. Her build. You know about the scarlet fever?"

"No."

"I'm surprised your mother didn't tell you. Everyone got it. First the children and then the parents. It killed your father. Of course he was weak from the fall. It broke his back."

"And my mother?"

"Your mother, bless her soul, nursed him with never an angry word or a complaint. He was all she had left after she sent you girls away. A mistake, I thought. We all thought. Your father didn't know she was doing it. It must have broken his heart."

"Do you know what happened to her?"

Mrs. Feinhut looked surprised. "She went to live with you girls in the New World. She had been waiting for your father's back to get better so they could both go. After he died, she said she was going on her own."

A blackbird flew by us, so low and close I could have touched it. It sent a shiver down my spine.

When we were back in the car Oscar asked me why I hadn't told her that my mother had never arrived.

"I don't know what it would have achieved. I didn't have the energy."

We didn't talk much for most of the trip back. Oscar fed me poppy seed cookies and orange slices. He massaged the back of my neck.

"Do you want to stop?" he asked when we passed the farm where we had spent the night.

"No. It's good for me to be busy right now." I thought of Vera telling me the same thing when I found her cleaning the bathroom floor with a toothbrush. "Thank you, though."

"This has been hard on you."

"Yes."

He leaned over and put his hand on my cheek and stroked the same spot Mrs. Feinhut had. "When we get back to St. Petersburg, Anna," he said, "let's get married. A real commitment. For both of us."

* * *

I put on Oscar's favorite suit a week later. I had made an important decision and was going to the coffee house to tell him about it.

I wouldn't marry him, I had decided, but I would stay in St. Petersburg for another year to see if we could make it work. But he would have to make an effort. He would have to introduce me to the people at the meetings, to the people at the coffee house, to the translation people he worked with. Maybe we could make a go of it.

I took two Russian newspapers with me to the coffee house so I could work on my Russian if Oscar was late, as he often was. It was late July, about eight in the evening; the sky as bright as it had been at eight that morning, as bright as it had been for weeks. *Beliye Nochi*, Oscar had told me it was called, White Nights. Because St. Petersburg is so far north and so high, he said, the sun can't go below the horizon at this time of year. He said it was like a holiday for Russians. As I walked to the coffee house, I could see it was true.

The sunlight hadn't affected the length of the breadlines, but it was making a difference to the mood of the people in the lines. Instead of standing in a row with their faces down, shuffling forward inch by inch, the lines were sloppy now with people standing in groups, chatting, sitting on the roads, playing games with stones. Children were running around.

The coffee house was quieter than usual. I assumed most people wanted to be outside. On my way to our regular table, I passed two men I hadn't seen before. They were both in Cheka uniforms and had long greasy blond hair.

"Who's the whore?" one of them asked in Russian.

"Oscar's latest," was the answer. "His one-way ticket to America. Let's hope it works this time," and they both laughed.

My cheeks burning, I left the coffee house and went to the U.S. Embassy office.

Breathless by the time I got there, I opened the door to an almost-empty room. The filing cabinets were gone, as were four camelback leather chairs I had seen on my last visit. All that remained was a brown leather sofa with silver studs on the arms, a heavy mahogany desk, and a high-backed carved wooden chair behind it, where a slender young man I hadn't seen before was seated.

I walked up to him, my boots echoing on the marble. "I'd like to see Mason Tate," I said.

"Who may I say is calling?"

"My name is Anna Grieve."

"I'm afraid Mr. Tate is not here right now, Miss Grieve," the young man said. "May I give him a message and have him contact you when he is back?"

From the way he spoke, I assumed he was Russian, although it was hard to be certain. His English, like Oscar's, was perfect, formal and outdated.

"No," I said, "I'll wait," and sat down on the leather sofa.

"The office is closing in forty-five minutes," the young man said. "Mr. Tate won't be back tonight."

"Then I'll wait here until morning."

"I don't think that's allowed," he said. When I didn't respond he said it again.

I opened one of my newspapers.

Glancing back at me every few seconds, the young man walked to a black door behind him, his shoes now echoing on the floor. He came back a few moments later followed by a squat, middle-aged man in a brown double-breasted suit.

"Can I help you, Madame?" the older man asked.

"Yes. My name is Anna Grieve. I'm an American citizen. I live in Manhattan and I have to get back immediately. I believe my passport and transit papers are here. At least they should be."

"What is your name, please?" he asked, walking to the desk and pulling open a drawer.

"Anna Grieve," I repeated. "I know my file is here, somewhere."

The older man said something quietly to the younger man and they both started to rifle through the desk drawers.

"Where is Mr. Tate, please?" I asked.

His head still in a drawer, looking for my papers, the older man said, "I'm afraid that Mr. Tate is back in America—permanently."

I froze.

"I believe that your papers have arrived though," he continued, "but we have to find them and go over them. Can you come back in the morning?"

"No. I'll wait here. This office is considered American soil, is it not?"

"Yes. It is."

"Then I'll stay here until tomorrow morning."

"Are you in some kind of trouble, Madame?" he asked.

"I am."

"Can you tell me what it is?"

"Not exactly, but I need the protection of the U.S. government."

"Ah, well then," he said confidently, as if he could calm my fears with his attitude, "I'll walk you back to your residence and pick you up again in the morning. Please," he said and held his elbow out to me invitingly.

"I'm not leaving this office unless it's to get on a ship for the United States," I said and went back to the newspaper.

The two men looked at each other and retreated to the office at the back. They closed the door behind them. A few moments later, the younger man returned alone.

"We have sent a telegram to Mr. Tate," he said. "We should hear from him by morning if not before. I'll stay here with you overnight and we'll make a decision as soon we hear from Mr. Tate." He went back to his desk and sat down.

A few moments later the older man came out of his office carrying a brown worn briefcase. He walked past me without a glance or a word. I heard the door lock from outside.

"I have cake," the young man said after a few moments. "Would you like some?"

"No thank you."

After the young man ate his cake, he slid down on the high-backed chair behind the desk and fell asleep with his legs spread in front of him and his mouth open. I spent the night lying on the hard leather sofa. It had cracks and rips that caught on the fibers of my suit. At seven the next morning I heard a key in the lock and the man in the double-breasted suit walked in.

"I've heard from Mason Tate," he said. "We're putting you on the *Adelor*. It's a freighter we use to transport diplomats to and from the United States. Don't let the term freighter disturb you. It is very well appointed and will be nothing like your trip over here on the *Nymphe*. Come with me now please," he said, putting his arm out for me. "The *Adelor* leaves for New York in two hours."

• CHAPTER TWENTY-THREE •

Even though I was only gone for seven months, the Manhattan I came home to felt like a different place. The war was over, so was the recession—temporarily at least. We were on the brink of what we later called the Roaring Twenties, a freewheeling decade that changed America forever. Skirts went up. Morals went down. The Charleston replaced the waltz. Psychoanalysis replaced repression and all of white Manhattan it seemed discovered the jazz clubs of Harlem that I had learned to love with Cedric.

I was at one—Jimmy's Place on Broadway—the night women got the vote. Even the cops on the beat were pretending that prohibition didn't exist.

It was difficult not to think about Russia. You couldn't open a newspaper then without reading about the communists and the anarchists and aliens. The Red Scare was still very real. Emma Goldman had been deported a few months after I got home. Oscar was right about her continuing fight for the rights of the underdog.

I tried to see Esther after I got back but she was always too busy. With the Sanctuary, she said, or a dog shelter. I took her at her word and picked up where I had left off. The California Perfume Company gave me my old routes back. I continued to sell womb veils illegally and handed out Margaret's birth control pamphlets for a few more years. I stopped when she started promoting birth control to weed out undesirables and create a race of thoroughbreds.

* * *

I've never come to terms with my time in St. Petersburg, whether I was really one in a line of women that Oscar had been courting to get them to take him back to Manhattan. In my more self-indulgent moments I tell myself that staying there wasn't such a bizarre idea. I did, as the Count had pointed out to me when I was young, have a strong social conscience and Oscar's diatribes spoke directly to it.

In my more honest moments, I tell myself the truth. I was terribly attracted to the man: his size, his confidence, his passion. And as much as I hate to admit it, I was smitten with the way he looked after me. No one before him or since has ever done that.

* * *

One April morning, not quite a year after I arrived home, I opened what I realized was my last tube of Brylcreem and decided to walk to my barber for more. I knew that if I ran out and the rain continued, my hair would become a tangled mess.

It was a Thursday. I put on a light raincoat and pulled a burgundy waterproof cloche over my head. On the way, I looked in at the Gotham Book Mart on Forty-Fifth Street. It had opened shortly after I got back to Manhattan and had become an overnight sensation. I wasn't surprised. It was as much a salon for the literary avant-garde as it was a store for selling books. It specialized in poetry, literature, theater, art, music, and dance. It stocked out-of-print books and books that had been banned. Vera and I went there often for author readings and art exhibits. We'd seen George Gershwin there and Christopher Morley, one of my favorite journalists.

Walking around the store, fingering the current crop of new books, I noticed a display on a table called *Russian Poets in Exile*. I picked one up. It was about twenty Russian poets who had fled the country after the revolution.

I bought a copy, went home, made myself a pot of tea, and settled into the big wing chair in front of the fireplace with four McVitie and Price's Digestive Biscuits.

There were dramatic black-and-white pictures of the poets with each of their stories; some of them looked familiar. They had all fled their beloved homeland after the revolution. "The new man, the Bolshevik hero, is no longer a man at all," one of the poets said. "He is a brutal animal, intent on staying alive by following the rules of an evil machine."

I went to the window when I finished the book. It was dark and had stopped raining. I loved the city this way, quiet and wet and ready for spring. I thought about Russia again, about what I had seen, about Oscar.

The phone lifted me from my reverie. It was the Winnipeg police. Esther had abducted a baby and was in a psychiatric ward in a hospital in Winnipeg. I left for Winnipeg the next day and, ten days later, brought Esther home with me for long-term psychiatric care.

* * *

"Her behavior had been erratic for some time," Dr. Gordon Pleasance, president of the Ellis Street Sanctuary where Esther volunteered, told me. "Going into the nursery, lifting the babies out. That kind of thing. We chose to ignore it for a while."

We were sitting across from each other at a gray metal table in an interview room at the Winnipeg Police Station, undrinkable cups of coffee we'd both pushed to the center of the table in front of us.

"We had no idea that she was ill, that she was even capable of abducting a baby," he said.

I had no idea either. She always sounded so in control when I talked to her on the phone after I got home from Russia. I always imagined her in her study, the sun streaming through the French doors, Licorice on a pillow at her feet.

It wasn't true. She had closed up the house, rented a small apartment in St. Boniface, and had been living there for six months under the name of Mrs. Kace. I remembered that she had talked about moving to St. Boniface in one of her letters to me in Russia, but I had no idea she had followed through.

"Believe me when I tell you, Miss Grieve," Dr. Pleasance continued, "none of us underestimates the role your sister and your whole family have played with the Sanctuary. We wouldn't exist if it weren't for Countess Chernovski. I think it best, however, that Mrs. Kinnear take some time off."

As much as I wanted to go to the hospital to see Esther, I decided to postpone a visit until I had talked to the people who could fill me in on what had happened. I had a big decision to make. The Sanctuary would not make a complaint and the police would not press charges if I agreed to be responsible for Esther for two years and find her psychological care. If I didn't, she would be charged and placed in the hospital in Winnipeg until she was well.

The police were helpful. They made a room available, set up my appointments, and kept a steady stream of undrinkable coffee going.

I took mine to the washroom every time I went there and flushed it down the toilet. I didn't want them to think I was unappreciative.

When I wasn't at the police station, I took in the city. I even went to the house in which Esther and I had grown up. I didn't see anybody coming or going, but it looked to be in good repair and from what I could see, the Countess's conservatory was still in use. Lights were on, the windows were foggy.

* * *

"I didn't know she was going to take that baby, Miss," Joseph, the care-taker at the Sanctuary said, twirling his tweed cap in his hands.

"I should have had her sign in that night. I know that. I've certainly been there long enough to know that, but Mrs. Kinnear, your sister I mean, told me that Matron knew she was there, and I believed her. She was there for a file, she said. So I went back to my office and she went into the nursery and snatched that little blond girl. Her parents were all lined up. They were to come and get her the next day, I think."

He shook his head. "She's a good person, your sister, and everyone loves her. She found the mothers jobs, you know. Did you know? It must have been hard on her, having no family left, no children. I'm not saying, mind, that it was right for her to take that baby."

Reeling from the whole thing, I closed my eyes after that interview and woke up when the police escorted in Lily-Ann McInnis, the wait-ress who had discovered Esther with the baby.

"Shall I bring you fresh coffee?" the officer asked.

I declined.

Lily-Ann was twenty at most, long-legged and awkward. She reminded me of myself at that age.

"She came into Frère Dani almost every day with the baby for a take-out lunch and later a take-out dinner," Lily-Ann said. "She said she lived across from the park, that she and her husband had just moved here. The baby was beautiful. Always with a little hat so I didn't notice the forceps marks."

"The forceps mark?" I asked.

"Oh yes. If it hadn't been for that mark, I never would have connected her baby with the missing baby. The missing baby had a forceps mark from the delivery just below her hairline above her left eyebrow. You could see it on the posters around the city. I didn't connect the two until I saw the mark on Mrs. Kace's baby when she lost her dog."

I could barely keep up with the story. Had she really rented an apartment in St. Boniface under the name Mrs. Kace and looked after a baby there for two months? And what was this about her dog being lost? I asked Lily-Ann to explain.

"One day after my shift, I saw Mrs. Kace running down the street with her baby in her arms. She was yelling 'Licorice! Licorice!' Her hair was flying and she was upset. When I stopped her, she said she had lost her dog and I helped look for him. He was sitting in front of a bench at the park, licking his front paw, innocent as a lamb. The little girl didn't have one of her pretty bonnets on that day and I saw the mark on the baby's forehead."

"And you called the police?"

"Not right away. I was afraid of making a mistake and causing trouble when it might not have been the stolen baby at all. My aunt convinced me to go to the police. If she's innocent, my aunt said, no harm will be done. If that's someone else's baby, they deserve to have her back."

* * *

I didn't know it was Esther when I saw her at the hospital. She was sitting in a white wicker chair looking out a large bay window. She had a pink wrap around her shoulders, pilled and thin, nothing that she would ever have chosen. Her hair was pulled back and tied low with a black ribbon. It looked like it hadn't been washed for days. I went over and stood behind her.

"Esther," I said quietly. She didn't respond.

"Esther," I said again, "it's me, Bencke."

Still no response.

I crouched down beside her and touched her gently on the shoulder. She turned around slowly and looked at me with complete incomprehension.

"Esther, it's me, Bencke," I said. Her breath was sweet. She looked like a fragile old woman.

"Nurse," she called softly, looking past me to the doorway, fluttering one of her hands in front of her face.

"Esther," I said, holding back the tears, "it's me, Bencke. I'm going to take you home to Manhattan with me. Everything will be all right."

"Will it?" she asked, looking up at me at last, the look in her eyes so vulnerable it brought tears to mine. "I promise I won't be any trouble," she said.

• CHAPTER TWENTY-FOUR •

S pring has sprung, the grass is riz.
  I wonder where the boidie is.
The boid is on the wing.
But that's absoid. I always thought the wing was on the boid.

That ditty—which an old boyfriend of mine had erroneously told me was written by Ogden Nash—was going through my head as I walked through Gramercy Park on my way to a meeting with Esther's psychiatrist. She'd been seeing him twice a week for almost two years when he called and asked me to come in. I hadn't seen him since I'd hired him to work with Esther; I assumed he wanted to tie up any loose ends before her sessions ended and she went back to Winnipeg. I decided I would give myself enough time to walk through Gramercy Park before our meeting.

It was a private park—only local residents had keys—and although I didn't live in the area, I'd been given a key years earlier by a boyfriend who did.

It was a beautiful April day. It had snowed unexpectedly two days earlier but the temperature had since climbed so high that the snow was gone. The songbirds sounded giddy with relief, the same relief I was feeling at the thought of Esther going home.

I slid my heavy key into the old-fashioned wrought iron gate and stood back as two little boys on matching yellow scooters raced by me into the park. A nanny with a navy cape flying behind her rushed to keep up with them. The boys went to a little pond that hadn't been there the last time I was and put a toy ship in the water. Spring had definitely sprung.

* * *

Dr. Gershstein's office was at the south end of the park. He had two small rooms on the second floor of a tall, skinny brownstone. They were bright, uncluttered, totally unlike the other offices I had seen when I started looking for someone to help Esther.

The other psychiatrists' offices had had dark wood paneling and old-fashioned carpets and secretaries. Even the psychiatrists themselves looked like they had patterned themselves after daguerreotypes of psychiatrists at the turn of the century. They smoked pipes and had Van Dyke beards and tweed jackets with leather elbow patches.

Everything about Dr. Gershstein was different. His office walls were a warm red with a few childlike paintings in primary colors here and there. He had no secretary. He was young and alive when he opened the door to his inner sanctum and invited you in. When I talked about Esther, he seemed truly interested in her and sympathetic.

"Thank you for coming, Miss Grieve," he said this time, taking a folder from his desk and sitting across from me in a swivel chair. "It's a beautiful day out there."

"Yes. I stopped in the park. I've always loved it."

"Well," he said, opening the folder in his lap. "You're probably wondering why I called you here," he said.

"I assume it's to talk about Esther. Her time with you is nearly over."

"It is," he said. "And I do want to talk with you about your sister, but before I begin, I want you to know that I'm not doing this lightly. I take psychiatrist–patient confidentiality seriously. I don't normally discuss my patients with anyone but their parents or legal guardians. From what I understand, you have all the legal responsibilities of a guardian or a parent."

I told him I did.

"Good," he said. "Then let's begin. There are things I want to tell you about your sister—from a psychiatric point of view. Are you comfortable with that?"

* * *

Was I comfortable with that?

Should I have told him I wasn't comfortable with anything about Esther's living with me, that I felt like I did when we were young, constantly holding my breath, waiting for the old signs that she was going under?

Should I have told him that I had turned my office into a bedroom for Esther and was working from a tiny room in the attic? That it was boiling in the summer and freezing in the winter and never got enough air no matter the season? Should I have told him that I was claustrophobic and that Licorice was with me most of the time, his doggy smell filling what little air there was?

Should I have told him that Esther had filled the fridge with meat substitutes and salt substitutes and vegetables made into tablets that she bought in a health food store in the Bronx run by Seventh-Day Adventists?

Should I have told him about the plumbing issue? Esther liked to take baths in the early hours when everyone else was sleeping. Unfortunately, the bathroom pipes knocked after midnight. My plumber had drained the pipes, changed the clamps, broken through the bathroom walls, replaced the cast iron pipes with galvanized iron. All at great expense, all to no avail. When I finally got up the courage to tell Esther that she was keeping everyone up, she was truly sorry, but didn't change her bathing hours. She started heating kettles on the stove and taking them down the hall to the bathroom, Licorice clicking along at her heels. She asked if this was a good solution and I said that of course it was. She was keeping only me awake now, not the whole house.

Then there was my love life, or lack of it since Esther had moved in. I was seeing an investment banker named Russell. I was fond of him and he of me. But Russell didn't like staying over with Esther there and I didn't want to leave her alone to spend the night at his place.

About six months into her stay, I started sneaking into her room when she was out with Licorice to read her journals. I hadn't seen any of the old signals that used to frighten me so. In fact, she was acting like she was on an extended holiday, but if something was going on, I wanted to know.

She wrote that she still missed Charles and the Count, how kind I was being, how much she liked Vera. She wrote that Manhattan overwhelmed her at first, but that she was getting used to it. She wrote that she was concerned about Mackenzie King becoming prime minister of Canada because people said he was anti-Semitic. She also worried that a man named Adolph Hitler had become the leader of the National

Socialist Workers' Party in Germany. She wrote several times that that she was looking forward to going home.

* * *

"Are you comfortable with that, Miss Grieve?" Dr. Gershstein repeated. "With hearing what I have to tell you about my diagnosis and my suggestions for future therapy?"

"Yes. I think I am." I was apprehensive but interested.

"Good." He opened the file on his lap. "Has Esther told you anything about our sessions?"

"Only in general terms. She says she's comfortable with you, that you seem to understand her."

"I'm glad to hear that. Now, forgive me for what I'm about to ask you, Miss Grieve, but are you sure your sister abducted a baby?"

I almost laughed out loud. In the time that Esther had been with me, I had wondered myself whether it had really happened. I couldn't imagine Esther walking into the Sanctuary and lifting a baby out of its crib. I couldn't imagine her renting an apartment under an assumed name and living there on her own, taking care of an infant.

When I brought the subject up with her, which wasn't often, she looked like a startled fawn. It was the same look she used to get on her face when she'd forgotten where she had been or what she had done.

She didn't remember any of it. As far as she was concerned, she was in Manhattan with me seeing Dr. Gershstein to cope with the grief she was still experiencing after Charles's and the Count's deaths.

* * *

"I never saw the baby myself, Dr. Gershstein," I said, "and I never saw Esther take it, but I'm as certain as I can be, yes, that it happened. She was found with the baby in her arms."

"I understand."

He wrote a few things down and continued. "Your sister has told me a lot about her life, Miss Grieve, at least what she can remember of it. What she *doesn't* remember is the crux of what I want to talk with you about today. But first let me ask you a few things. Do you know that she's obsessed with anti-Semitism? She seems to be afraid that she'll be found out and someone will hurt her."

"I wouldn't have called it obsessed," I said. "I know she doesn't want anyone to know she's Jewish."

"Do you know about her out-of-body experiences?"

"I know she used to get headaches and felt like she was living on another plane. Is that what you mean by out-of-body experiences?"

"Yes. That's a good example." He made a few more notes.

"Are you aware that she sometimes hurts herself? She pricks herself with a hatpin. The external pain then takes over for a while from the internal pain."

I shuddered at the image of Esther hurting herself.

"I'm sorry, Miss Grieve," he said. "I don't mean to upset you. I just think it's important that you understand what your sister has been dealing with."

"I appreciate that. Please go on."

"She's forgotten how to play the piano. Has she told you that?"

I was shocked. She hadn't told me that, but it explained why, when I offered to rent or buy a piano for her stay with me, she had declined.

"It happened about eight years ago," he said. "She explained that Charles asked her to play the piano one day and she didn't remember that she had ever played."

He leaned forward and closed his file.

"Here is the crux of the issue, Miss Grieve. I think that your sister has a disorder called dissociation. Have you heard of it?"

"No."

"I'm not surprised. It was recognized as early as the sixteenth century but rejected as witchcraft. A French psychotherapist named Janet legitimized it recently and named it dissociation. Most psychiatrists dismiss it. I don't. I think your sister is a classic case. When I look at her presentation, it's the only diagnosis that makes any sense. Let me explain. May I get you a glass of water?"

"Please."

He waited until I had drained the glass and put it down. "May I go ahead?"

"Yes."

"Please interrupt if you have questions."

I nodded.

"Most of the people I see suffer from simple neuroses, which are caused by repression," he said. "Do you know what repression is?"

"I think so," I said. "It's when you don't allow yourself to feel an emotion."

"Exactly. Neurotic people tend to deal with their pain in ritualistic ways, if they deal with it at all. They make sure they don't step on sidewalk cracks. They open letters in the same way all the time. That kind of thing. Given time and psychiatric support many of them go on to lead healthier lives. It's not that simple with dissociation. With repression, the trauma is blocked *from* the contents of the mind and can be accessed. With dissociation, the trauma is blocked by the actual *structure* of the mind. We don't know why it is, but it is. As far as we know, dissociation is caused by a violent trauma or series of traumas when the patient is very young, usually sexual in nature, often repeated. Do you know if something sexually traumatic, some kind of assault, happened to your sister when she was young?"

It was four o'clock. Traffic was building on the street below us. People hailing taxis, car doors slamming. Children yelling on their way home from school. I remembered my dream in the root cellar.

"It's possible, Dr. Gershstein," I said, thinking about my dream. "All my life I've had a dream of being in the root cellar in our home in Russia. I was four or five and could hear Esther and Mamma screaming upstairs."

"Was there anything unusual going on around that time?"

"Yes. Of course. We were living in Russia. The tsar had just been assassinated. I'm sure you know about it. We were suddenly overrun with Russian soldiers, intent on punishing Jews for his murder."

"So Esther could have been sexually assaulted then, perhaps raped."

Just like that, no warning, it all clicked into place.

"Yes. She could have."

"May I go on?" he asked gently after a few moments. "I know this must be difficult for you."

"Yes."

"Did you ever tell Esther about these dreams?"

"I did. She said it was just that—bad dreams."

"She would say that because she wouldn't remember the incident. That's the thing with dissociatives. They have no access to the initial trauma or any other trauma that has happened since that triggers the initial trauma."

"What do you mean?"

"I mean that if something happened today, something completely unrelated to the sexual assault, it could trigger the memory of that assault and she would forget that incident as well."

"I'm not following you."

"Well, if the man or men who assaulted her had rifles and boots, just the sight of rifles and boots could bring up the memory. She would have to shut down completely—the past and the present—to maintain her equilibrium. She goes into an altered state of consciousness. Does that help?"

It did. It didn't. I thought about the times I'd seen her that way.

"How long does she stay shut down for?" I asked.

"Minutes, hours, days. It depends. In the case of the baby, months. In the case of the piano and the rape, forever."

"But she remembers her abortion," I said. "And she remembers Charles's illness and death and she knows exactly when each of her dogs died."

"There's nothing logical about what will trigger the initial incident in her mind and what won't. It could be triggered by something as inconsequential as a color or a smell. Nobody can predict that."

"Can anything be done?" I asked.

"There is no traditional therapy and there are no drugs, I'm sorry to say. So much of the psychiatric community doesn't even acknowledge it as legitimate. But there are alternative treatments that I would like to try with her. I honestly don't know if they'll work, but I'm willing to try them.

"I need to know if you're willing to carry on as her guardian. She can go home if she chooses. The two years are up and I don't think she'll be a danger to anyone back in Winnipeg. I don't believe her kidnapping the baby had anything to do with her dissociation although her forgetting about it certainly did. I believe the kidnapping was a psychotic break caused by the death of her husband and then her father. I've told the psychiatrist in Winnipeg that."

"Have you told Esther about your diagnosis and suggested these treatments?"

"Not yet. I wanted to make sure that you're willing to have her continue living with you. If you are, I'll tell her at our next session."

"May I think about it for a few days?"

"Of course."

"Is there anything I should do in the meantime?"

"Do exactly what you already seem to be doing—loving her and supporting her. She counts on you a great deal. I assume you know that. Don't pressure her. Don't pursue the baby issue, or any other issue that makes her uncomfortable. Your sister has spent her life building intricate compensation techniques to keep the initial trauma from her conscious mind. It's a survival mechanism, and it appears to be working well for her most of the time. But she has to be able to escape to safety. If she can't, it could have tragic consequences."

I stopped in the park on the way home to think about what it would be like to have Esther staying with me longer. A young man and woman approached the gate from outside. He took out a key and opened the gate, pulled it back, and walked through with his arm around his girlfriend. When they had gone a few feet, she put her hand on his cheek and said something to him. He ran back and checked that the gate was properly closed before joining her.

I zigzagged my way back home slowly, rubble and jackhammers and detour signs everywhere. It felt like they were inside my head.

I was washing a few dishes in the kitchen sink a couple of days later, enjoying the warmth of the water on my hands, wondering what to do, when Esther came home from her session with Dr. Gershstein and announced that she was going back to Winnipeg. She wanted to start her life again. She seemed so confident, so full of hope about the future.

I felt a surge of relief. Dr. Gershstein had told me her life was working well for her most of the time. I decided it was time to get mine working again too.

Anybody watching us at the train station the day she left would have misjudged the situation. Esther was happy and excited. She kept kissing Licorice on his nose and telling him he would be home soon in his very own garden. When the conductor yelled "All aboard," I started to blubber. Esther put her arms around me and rubbed my back, kissed my cheek, told me it would be all right.

A few days later, she called. "Everything is familiar but brand new at the same time." Her voice was so full and happy.

"So it feels good?"

"Yes. The property managers did a wonderful job while I was gone. The place was spotless. They took the covers off the furniture and washed the windows and cleaned out the fireplaces. They even bled the radiators," she said. "I know a great deal more about plumbing now than I did before." And then she laughed her lovely tinkly laugh. "I'd forgotten how much I love my things, Bencke—my porcelain angels, the artwork, my books, the silver."

* * *

After an initial flurry of letters and phone calls, our correspondence got spotty again. Esther started taking cooking lessons, developed an interest in modern art, went to galleries and plays and concerts, met her few friends for lunch. She was invited to dinner parties where she told me there was often a single man of her age. A few called afterwards, but she wasn't interested in getting involved.

Two years later she started volunteer work at a local library, reading to youngsters after school. I worried initially about her being with small children. I even called Dr. Gershstein to see if I should alert the police, but he told me not to worry; that he was certain the abduction wasn't part of her pathology.

I run up those library stairs twice a week, she wrote, *not sure who is more excited about my being there—the children or me. There are six or eight of them sitting cross-legged in a semi-circle when I arrive, fidgeting with pleasure, waiting for me to pull up my little chair and complete the circle. Their parents can't afford nannies or governesses so they come here after school for a few hours, so beautiful and innocent with their little faces turned up to me.*

Now and then she asked if I could think of any good children's books that she might read aloud. I suggested a few and sent her my copy of *The Happy Family*, a book I'd found years earlier in an antique store and fallen in love with.

• CHAPTER TWENTY-FIVE •

In August of 1929, my boyfriend, Russell, told me to sell my stocks. "Everything?" I asked.

"Everything."

The market had been fluctuating wildly since March but I'd been reluctant to part with anything. My shares—a Norwegian publishing house, a German automotive supplier, and made-right-here in America Leaf Brands candies—had made me a wealthy woman. But I knew Russell was right, so I sold everything except my candy stocks. Even if the fluctuations continued, I rationalized, people would continue to buy candy, just like they had continued to buy my California Perfume Company products during the war.

In September Russell told me to take my cash out of the bank.

"Everything?"

"Everything."

"And put it where?" I asked. "Under the mattress?"

"It would be safer there than in the bank."

On October 29, the market crashed.

I drove to the stock exchange to sell my candy shares but couldn't get within six blocks of it. Cars were everywhere: angled wildly on the road, on the sidewalks, up against the buildings. Hundreds of people were climbing around and over them to get to the exchange doors, yelling, waving their shares above their heads. Mounted policemen with batons were at the exchange doors holding them back. I went home and, like the rest of the country, sat glued to my radio.

Twelve million people lost their jobs. One thousand six hundred and sixteen banks went bankrupt. Twenty-three thousand people committed suicide. And that was just the first year.

Bread lines and soup kitchens sprang up. They weren't like the lines in St. Petersburg. There, people had stood facing forward, silent, bent, beaten. Here families pulled up in their cars, slapped For Sale signs on the windshields, and walked up and down the sidewalks with sandwich boards saying they would work for food or lodging. They sat on curbs, chatted, shared their lunches, stories, and tips on where to find work.

The dust storms hit the Great Plains the next year and displaced seventy-five percent of the topsoil and another three and a half million people, Hector Finlayson and his family among them. I wasn't home when Hector and his boys stopped in front of our house. Vera told me about them when I got home later that day. Their dusty black pickup truck had pulled up in front of the house at about one that afternoon. A tall, lanky man stepped out, took a blue and white checkered kerchief from his shirt pocket, and ran it over his face. He went to the other side of the truck and opened the passenger door. His six-year-old twins, Charlie and Andrew, tumbled out followed by their three-legged border collie, Tripod. Vera watched from the front window as the dog relieved himself against a tire and the lanky man wiped the boys' faces with his kerchief. He then went to the back of the truck, opened a metal box, took three root beers from it, and handed two to the boys. He then poured some water into a bowl for the dog. The boys and their dad leaned back against the truck, heads back as they sucked back their drinks.

Their farm had been hit by a dust storm that he said was like a plague, the air so thick and black you couldn't see your hand in front of your face. Hector's wife, Sylvia, had gone out back to bring the chickens into the house and never came back. He found her dead, two days later, between the barn and the house.

"I asked them in for lunch, Anna," Vera told me when I found them in the kitchen. "I knew you wouldn't mind."

* * *

By 1935, I had a full house.

We put mattresses in the living room and dining room and the main floor library. People paid what they could, did what they could, and stayed as long as they needed to.

One night stands out in my memory as one of the sweetest nights of my life. It was June, about seven in the evening. I had just finished my dinner in my apartment upstairs. The kitchen window was open and the air was soft. I could hear the thwack of a bat hitting a softball from the park down the street. I could hear my downstairs tenants; there were eight of them at that time, pushing their chairs back from the kitchen table and clearing up.

They would soon be starting to sing, I knew. They would sit around the kitchen table, lean against the walls and sit on the floor. I would join them soon, not yet. I knew that if I went down before the music started, they would insist that I take their seats and offer me their precious cigarettes. I didn't like being treated like the landlady even if I was one.

Tommy Tommasson started, strumming, humming, tuning his voice like an instrument. Chairs stopped scraping, everyone became quiet. I could imagine Tommy with his eyes closed, his nostrils flaring, his big hands on the guitar as he filled the room with the longing lyrics to the song that had become synonymous with the Depression.

I have a recording of "Brother Can You Spare a Dime" by Rudy Vallee. It became popular when the bottom fell out of the market, but Rudy Vallee's version has never moved me the way Tommy's did. I listened for Ben's harmony, but it wasn't there. Maybe he wasn't back from work yet. I knew Vera would save dinner for him.

* * *

Ben had come to Manhattan from Kansas after he lost his wife and three-year-old son to the dust storms in Kansas. He was a cattle farmer and his wife taught primary school and raised goats.

He and Vera met at the bakery where Vera worked and a few weeks later, she asked me if he could move in with her. I was surprised. She had dated now and then, but I'd never seen her serious about anyone. He stayed for about ten years, keeping Vera happy and the house in perfect repair. There was nothing he couldn't fix or replace. He asked Vera to go back to Kansas with him when the dust storms ended. He missed farming and the land. But she didn't want to leave Manhattan. They spend holidays together now and do some traveling but when Ben's not around, I have her to myself and we both love it.

• CHAPTER TWENTY-SIX •

I walk through Esther's house one last time before I leave. I take a few photographs from her bookcase and the silver filigreed Austrian perfume bottle that the Countess gave her for her fifteenth birthday. I'd always loved it. Everything else will be sold at an estate sale, the proceeds going to the animal shelter Esther supported.

The funeral had been quiet: the minister, a few of Esther's society friends, some people from the library and from the Sanctuary, including Dr. Pleasance and the caretaker, Joseph.

I was surprised to see Inspector McHugh at the gravesite when the taxi dropped me off. He was watching two burly men in toques and gloves break through the ice with hatchets and shovels.

I walked up to him. "Thank you for coming. I appreciate it."

"I'm glad I could make it."

My heart leapt when Nathaniel arrived a few moments after the service began. He stood a few feet behind me, smiled when I turned to him and nodded.

The minister said a few words about Esther's untimely passing but spoke mainly about her life, the people that she loved and had loved her, about how she would always be remembered for her volunteer work.

When the service was over, Nathaniel asked me if I had a few moments.

I looked at my watch. "I don't, Nathaniel. I'm sorry. I have to get back to the hotel."

"I can drive you there," he said, gesturing to the parking lot with his head. "My car is over there."

"I can't, Nathaniel."

"I found her," he started. "She's a teacher in—"

I looked down and shook my head. "Don't."

"Don't you want to know?"

"No."

Inspector McHugh was standing a few feet away. He stepped forward. "Shall I leave, Miss Grieve, or would you like me to drive you back to the hotel?"

"Please, Inspector," I said. "I'd like that very much."

I turned to Nathaniel and looked into his soft brown eyes for what I knew would be the last time. "Thank you for coming to the funeral. Thank you for having the courage to do what I didn't. Thank you for telling me the truth."

* * *

I have a private compartment for the trip back. I put my overnight case and a large shopping bag with my warm winter gear in the overhead compartment, wondering why I bothered to bring it back with me. I'll never use it again.

I sit down and swing my legs up on to the seat so I can look out the window.

"The newspapers have printed the story about your sister," Inspector McHugh said when he drove me to the hotel from the funeral. "I was wondering if her death could have had anything to do with If Day?"

I was surprised. "Why would you think that?"

"A neighbor of mine's father had a mild stroke when he saw Nazi soldiers marching into the civic office."

"But she didn't see If Day," I said, confused. "She never made it past the train station."

"There was a lot of If Day activity there too," he said, reaching into the backseat of his car for a newspaper folded open at an inside page. "I didn't know it until I saw this. Here. You can read it on the train."

The story is about Esther—a socialite and philanthropist, they called her—who died on If Day in what the police confirmed was a suicide. There's a picture of a man identified as Sergeant Philip Lerdin of the Royal Winnipeg Air Rifles, one of the thousands of If Day volunteers. With the scar on his cheek and his Nazi uniform, he sure looks like the real thing to me, as do the dozens of other Nazis stopping passengers as they get off the train. A Nazi flag is waving from the station, a loud-speaker beside it. The story says it was tuned to the station the Nazis had commandeered to tell the city Winnipeg was now under Nazi rule and had been renamed Himmlerstadt.

The train starts moving, rocking me back and forth, my knees hitting and then leaving the soft side panel.

I can imagine Esther getting off the train; her overnight case in one hand, her Saks hatbox in the other, looking forward to seeing Licorice and the new man in her life.

I can't allow myself to imagine what she felt when she was confronted with soldiers, helmets, jackboots, rifles.

"She has to be able to escape to safety," Dr. Gershstein had said so many years ago. "If she can't it could have tragic consequences."

* * *

I fall asleep when the rhythm becomes steady, a deep dreamless sleep that consumes me as the days pass. When I'm not sleeping, I'm remembering my beautiful sister: on the swing in Podensk, her hair sailing behind her like a blond flag; in front of a group of volunteers at the Sanctuary, so happy that I'm there to witness her success. I feel her arms around me at Grand Central Station when I start to cry because she's leaving, telling me quietly that it will be all right.

I'm free of Esther at last, and it breaks my heart.

Three days later the train rattles through a corridor of tall industrial buildings peeking through the morning fog. The Harlem tenements will be next; laundry stiff on clotheslines, someone leaning over a fire escape, stealing a few moments with a cigarette. I close my eyes and wait for the click of the flying switch as the brakeman uncouples the engine from the rest of the cars, and we glide silently, seamlessly, into Grand Central Station.

• AUTHOR'S NOTE •

While the story line and the main characters in this novel are fictitious, many of the people, places and events are based on historical fact—the most important one being If Day, which was the inspiration for the novel.

• ACKNOWLEDGEMENTS •

Thank you to Kathryn Cole and Margie Wolfe of Second Story Press for seeing the promise in my manuscript; to Wendy Thomas, my editor, for helping me fulfill that promise; to John Gillis for guiding me through the streets of Manhattan; and to Kurt, with gratitude and love, for his unwavering support.

• ABOUT THE AUTHOR •

Heather Chisvin is the daughter of Russian immigrants who moved to Winnipeg to avoid the pogroms of the early 20th century. She is a journalist, a radio and television documentary producer, an advertising copywriter and a former teacher at the Ontario College of Art and Design. This is her first work of fiction. She lives in Port Hope, Ontario.